Praise for Avery Flynn's Books:

"Sexy and sassy... Avery Flynn brings it all."—*Carly Phillips, NY Times Bestselling Author*

"This book is so good you won't want to put it down."—*Harlequin Junkie, Enemies on Tap*

"Flynn intertwines fashionistas and fighters in book two of this heavily talked-about series and she'll leave readers breathless by the time they reach the heart-pounding finish."—*4.5 starts Top Pick, RT Book Reviews, This Year's Black*

Flynn knows her sass and sex ... sheer naughty fun!"—*Into the Fire author Amanda Usen, Betting the Billionaire*

"I loved this story."—*Darynda Jones, NY Times Bestselling Author, Jax and the Beanstalk Zombies*

"...Thrilling, funny passionate and even contains a few tips to keep the fashion police away from your doorstep."—*RT Book Reviews, High-Heeled Wonder*

Hollywood on Tap

By Avery Flynn

Visit Avery's website at www.averyflynn.com.

Edited by KC

Cover design by Babski Creative Studio

ISBN 978–0–9908335–0–5 (digital)

ISBN 978–0–9908335–1–2 (print)

Manufactured in the United States of America

First Edition November 2014

To everyone who is a little bit sweet and a little bit sour – may you always find just the right mix of the two.

Chapter One

Five Months Ago

Kellwood, Missouri

There was a difference between making love and fucking. Both were fun and—hopefully—got you to the same place, but they were as different as sweet and sour. Natalie Sweet had done a lot of the first, but only a little of the second and as she silently slid one leg from between the sheets, she realized she wanted more.

The wood floor's early morning cold burned her toes as she eased her weight off the king–sized bed, wincing when the man sprawled across it grumbled in his sleep.

She froze.

Natalie held her position and her breath until Max rolled over, revealing the Lincoln State University bulldog mascot tattooed on his left shoulder. Even as she was in the process of sneaking out like a naked thief in the night, she couldn't help but sigh at the head football coach's muscular back. Lincoln may be an NCAA Division Two school, but

Max had a Division One body and the hunky brain to go with it.

And if she wasn't a half–nuts Sweet from Salvation, Virginia, she would have taken him up on his post–coital offer. But she hadn't...couldn't. Max was a good guy, but he wasn't ever going to be *her* guy. The sex was amazing, but that's all it was for her—sex.

She swept her neatly folded pink cardigan, cream skirt, and taupe underwear up off the chair, scooped her black Mary Janes from the floor, and clutched them to her chest as she tiptoed to the bedroom door.

"Not even a goodbye kiss on the cheek?" Max tsk–tsked. "And you're usually so particular about protocol."

Natalie halted mid–step, her nose scrunched up and shoulders hunched. "I didn't want to wake you," she managed to squeak out.

He sighed. "I didn't mean to freak you out last night."

Yep. They were going to have this conversation. Goodie, goodie gumdrops. "You didn't." She turned around and the you–are–totally–full–of–shit expression on his face made her laugh out loud. "Okay. You did. But it's not you. Really. It's me."

"Wow." Max rubbed the scruff on his chin. "Normally I'm the one saying that line."

She couldn't do this naked. It just wasn't proper. Natalie dressed in thirty–four seconds; she knew because she'd time it repeatedly in high school until she'd eliminated every unnecessary move and shaved every extra second from the action.

Once clothed, she put on her dark–rimmed glasses and ran her fingers across her pearl necklace.

Dealing with anxiety had been a daily battle that she'd waged for most of her life. Thanks to Dr. Kenning, a shitload of yoga, and her devotion to creating order from chaos, she hadn't had a panic attack in years.

Comforted—as always—by her personal talisman, Natalie faced Max. "You are an amazing guy—"

"Ouch." He slapped his palm over his heart as if he'd been shot. "Friend zoned."

"You're such a goof." Which was one of the things she really liked about Max. He always made her laugh and he was completely direct, which was what led to this conversation in the first place. No one ever said the truth was comfortable. "We've been friends with benefits for...what...three months?"

He nodded. "Sounds about right."

She squared her shoulders. Now to lay it all out in a straightforward manner, just like during a client presentation about an efficiency strategy. She could do this. She had a black belt in compartmentalizing. "And we both came into it with our eyes open. I was totally honest and upfront about my disinterest in a relationship, as were you."

"Yes. The efficiency expert explained it all very methodically, although I was disappointed in the lack of a PowerPoint." Max said it with a smile, but there was an underlying hurt in his tone.

Guilt pricked her conscience because she really did care about Max. This was why she had always separated sex from any feeling beyond companionship. It got messy, and messy things were, by definition, illogical and disorderly. Two things that had always given Natalie cold sweats and psychological tremors.

"I didn't realize something had changed for you," she said.

"But not for you."

Her shoulders drooped. "Not for me." God, she wished she had a different answer.

Max scrubbed at his buzz–cut black hair as if he were washing out the past few months. "Is it not for you just with me or not for you with anyone?"

"I don't know, but I need to find out." It was past time, really.

He wrapped the soft blue sheet around his lean hips and strutted over to her, every inch of him looking as though he'd just stepped off the professional gridiron a month ago instead of five years. Damn. He was a walking orgasm and she had just turned down his proposal to date exclusively. Maybe there *was* something to the idea that all the Sweets were born with a self–destructive crazy gene.

"Change is a bitch." Max tucked a finger under her chin and tilted her face up so she had no choice but to look into his kind brown eyes. "Don't ever let her see you sweat."

"That wouldn't be very productive." Her voice wobbled with regret. Max's only sin was wanting more than her firmly boxed–up heart could give him.

"And everyone knows you won't put up with that." He brushed his lips across her forehead in a petal–soft kiss before smacking her ass like a football player about to storm the field. "Now get out of here before I drag you back into bed for goodbye sex."

Natalie held it together for the two minutes and fourteen seconds it took her to exit Max's apartment, cross the parking lot, and barricade herself behind her Honda Civic's locked doors. Only then did she give in to the tremble shaking her bottom lip and rest her forehead against the cold steering wheel.

For once, she didn't count the seconds as her shoulders shook and tears rolled down her cheeks.

Eventually the wetness dried, exhaustion replaced the shaking, and her composure returned.

"Whining and whimpering never solved anything." She pulled a tissue from the box kept in the glove compartment and patted it under her eye. She took a steadying breath before hooking her fingers in her pearl necklace and repeating her mantra. "See a problem. Fix a problem. There's a process for everything."

But what was the solution when the problem was her?

She glanced down at her phone to reread the text her older sister, Miranda, had sent yesterday. Well, older by all of three minutes. The same amount of time she was older than her little sister, Olivia. She brought up the message.

MIRANDA: THIS PLACE IS A TWENTY–FIVE ON A TEN POINT NIGHTMARE SCALE. I NEED AN EFFICIENCY EXPERT TO HELP GET THE BREWERY ONLINE. ANY RECOMMENDATIONS FOR FOLKS IN THE AREA WHO WON'T KILL MY BUDGET?

Her Uncle Julian, who'd left her and her sisters a worn–down craft brewery when he died, had sworn all the threes in the triplets' lives were good luck. If they were, she'd yet to experience it.

Her fingers stilled on her pearl necklace.

Salvation.

Maybe it wasn't *what* the solution to her problem was, but *where*.

If she were researching the source of her aversion to relationships, starting at the beginning made sense. For added value, she'd get to see her older sister and could help put the brewery back on the path to profitability. It was a win–win.

Turning the key in the ignition, Natalie started organizing her schedule in her head. None of the clients at her fledgling consulting firm needed her on location. She could as easily streamline their systems from Salvation, Virginia, as she could from Kellwood, Missouri.

She pulled out onto the street, invigorated by the prospect of a shiny new problem to fix and finally finding a solution to an old one.

Chapter Two

Present Day

Salvation, Virginia

At times like this, Sean O'Dell—movie star in hiding—almost wished he'd never left Hollywood and the millions sitting untouched in the bank.

If he could make it across the Sweet Salvation Brewery to the walk–in cooler in time, he could hide behind the crates of hops until Natalie Sweet left. Worst case scenario, he'd ditch the stubborn woman in the stacks of burlap bags filled with malt.

He'd purposefully ordered the staff to arrange them out of alphabetical order just to annoy the efficiency expert always nipping at his heels. The micromanaging menace could never go near them without stopping a staff member to help her put the bags to rights. He laughed, but didn't slow his breakneck pace through the brewery.

Hooking a left turn at the brew kettle, he pulled his Southeast Brewers Invitational baseball hat lower and hustled toward the cooler.

"Yo, brewmaster, hold up, man," the brewery's delivery driver hollered from the open bay door.

Sean didn't check his speed. "Nope."

"But your shadow–" The words faded into background noise when Sean made a left at the bottling station.

Punctual to the hundredths of a second, the bane of his existence marched out the door at 5:05 every day without fail. If he could make it undiscovered for the next ten minutes, he'd have until six tomorrow morning blissfully free of her clipboard, her flowcharts, her spreadsheets, and her plans to change everything about the brewery that he loved. Not to mention Natalie's big blue eyes, the stubborn tilt of her chin, and the curves she tried–and failed–to hide underneath cardigans the color of carnival cotton candy.

The question of exactly how fast, or slow, he could unfasten all those little pearly buttons haunted him as he lay in bed at night and in his morning shower–exactly the kind of thoughts he should not be having about the woman who signed his paychecks.

The walk–in cooler stood twenty feet away.

So frickin' close he could practically smell the flowery green hops and feel them crumble in his palms.

The weight on his chest eased with each step. He was going to close out the day without having yet another conversation with Natalie about lean manufacturing or whatever the hell system the people at Toyota invented.

She'd been hounding him all day to sit down with her and go over her crazy–ass plans to streamline the brewery process. As if the craft and creativity of making beer could be distilled down to numbers on a spreadsheet. The woman was as annoyingly persistent as she was hot—both were a distraction he didn't need in his life right now, not with the Southeast Brewers Invitational coming up.

But for the next thirteen hours, he wouldn't have to hear any of her harebrained recommendations. He reached for the cooler's door handle and turned it, noticing as he did so that it wasn't latched.

He yanked open the door before his brain processed the ants dancing up his spine.

The motion triggered the cooler's sensor–activated overhead lights. His gut dipped and he clenched his jaw.

Natalie stood shivering on the other side of the cooler's threshold, clutching her damn clipboard to her chest.

He stopped cold. "What in the hell are you doing here?"

"Waiting for you in your favorite hiding spot." Her teeth chattered. "Do you really think I don't know your secrets?"

God knew exactly how long she'd been lying in wait for him, but it was enough time for her button nose to turn red and her glasses to frost over. His gaze slid to the right. The temperature gage read twenty–six.

A smarter man would have shut the door and walked away, let her deal with the consequences of spending time in the cooler without a coat. But no one—from his asshole of a father to his always–hungry–for–more agent to his on–set teachers—had ever accused him of having an overabundance of brains.

Instead, he whipped off his thick hoodie and pulled it over her head. Not bothering to get her arms through the sleeves, he wrapped her up—clipboard and all—inside its fleece warmth. The hood drooped over her head, covering everything down to her nose. Before she could squeak out a noise over the chattering of her teeth, he wrapped an arm around her narrow waist and tossed her over one shoulder like a sack of grain. Her cold seeped into him, pouring over his body and making him shiver.

"P–p–put me down." She made a halfhearted attempt to wriggle free.

"No." He spun around and kicked the cooler door shut with his boot heel.

"This is unseemly."

Her body may be half a degree away from being a snow cone, but holding her like this had him running a few degrees warmer. "Yep."

"You can't just carry me around like this," Natalie huffed against his lower back. "I'm your boss."

"I can and you are." But he was bound to forget that last part if she kept squirming against him. Hell, he couldn't seem to remember that fact while he was alone at night staring at his bedroom ceiling and imagining how those damn little buttons would open under his touch.

He thought he'd made good time on his first trip across the brewery when he was trying to escape her. He was wrong. Busting ass to make it to his office—the warmest place in the building—without half the staff seeing him carting around the brewery's shivering co–owner over one shoulder had him hustling through his office door in half his earlier time.

"If you don't put me down right now, I'm going to—" Her pert ass hitting the chair stopped whatever threat was about to come out.

Sean crossed over to his desk and circled behind it, figuring the oak and the stacks of papers and dirty coffee cups covering it would offer him some protection—but maybe not enough, judging by the fire snapping in her blue eyes behind her defrosted glasses.

"You monosyllabic Neanderthal, I am not some little helpless female who can't walk across the brewery."

He shrugged. "I did what was needed."

"What the what?" She dropped the clipboard from beneath the hoodie and shoved her arms through the its sleeves before rubbing her hands up and down her arms to warm them. "That doesn't even make sense."

Sean doubted there were half–crazed mules more stubborn than Natalie Sweet. "If I hadn't, you would have stayed in that cooler, freezing your ass off until you'd said everything you wanted to say—which, by the way, is usually more words that most people use in a year."

Well, definitely more than he did, since that speech he'd just given had used up his allotted speaking time for the next week.

She blinked in surprise before immediately recovering her ire. "It was the most logical place to wait for you. You don't think I realize you've been ditching me every chance you could get? Anyway, I would have stepped outside the cooler." She paused. "Eventually."

He snorted.

"Well, you can't argue it didn't work because we're together now and I have the flowcharts that I need your input on. It would be wasteful not to take advantage of the situation."

"Tomorrow." He grabbed his keys from off his desk.

"Why are you so dead set against securing the brewery's future?"

Sean dropped his keys and shuffled through the paper pile in the middle of the desk. It took a second—okay, a few minutes—but he finally found the printed brochure for the Southeast Brewers Invitational, which he shoved across the desk toward Natalie.

She leaned forward to read it. "Breweries go head to head with one crowned champion in each of ten beer styles." Natalie looked up. "You think winning a competition would be better for the brewery than giving it a solid operational foundation?"

"Winning will do a lot more for Sweet Salvation Brewery than your four–billion–point plan will." Certainty as solid as a concrete block firmed his spine and filled him with confidence. "I'm going to make a beer that is going to blow those little buttons right off your sweater."

Natalie's sisters could tease her for the pearl necklace she always wore and she'd roll her eyes. People in Salvation could mock her for her family's wild, lawless history and she wouldn't even let it put a pause in her step. But to question her flowcharts? Mock her efficiency strategy?

Oh hell no, that shit did not stand.

"My plan has twenty–five points, thank you very much. Each of which is carefully thought out and considered utilizing the best manufacturing processes and customized to meet the needs of Sweet Salvation Brewery. All of which you would realize if you ever took five minutes to review my flowcharts." Her cheeks pulsed with the heat of a thousand fires, fueled by frustration and indignation. "You may like to think of this brewery as your own personal playground, where things happen willy–nilly so the creative process can work itself out, but it's not. There needs to be order. Direction. Documented processes."

Her voice cracked on the last word and her throat tightened, preventing her from expressing the rest of her outrage.

Damn it, this would not happen now.

Clamping her jaw shut tight, she inhaled a deep breath through her nose and kept her gaze locked on the crack in the wall above Sean's head. Her nose twitched and she swallowed hard as she blinked furiously to keep the tears at bay.

I will not give him the satisfaction.

"Are you okay?" Sean backed up slowly as if he had a roast chicken tied around his neck and was nose–to–nose with a rabid junkyard dog.

"I am..." The first hot tear slid down her cheek, followed by a thousand more. She could practically feel her nose enlarging and turning Rudolph red. She sniffled back snot. "Perfectly fine."

"Don't cry." He yanked open his center desk drawer and rifled through the contents. "I didn't mean to make you sad."

"I am not sad, you numbskull." She wiped the back of her hand across her cheek then pushed her glasses up the bridge of her nose. "I am really fucking mad."

"Then why are you crying?" He pulled a squashed mini–box of tissues from the drawer and held them out to her.

She swiped the box and yanked out a tissue. "It's a common physical reaction to extreme annoyance." Her voice wobbled like a deer in high heels and grew in volume with each word. "Especially when dealing with change–adverse jerks who think they're artists of alcohol and won't even consider for one damn second that all I'm trying to do is help."

"Artist of alcohol?" The corner of his mouth curled and he shook his head. It should have made him look smug. Instead it just emphasized his scruffy hotness. "I like that."

"Of course you do." Natalie patted her cheeks dry and wiped her nose. She knew from past experience that she was not a pretty crier. Blotchy face. Puffy eyes. Sniffly nose. It was a little late to be delicate now. She laid the tissue box on his desk.

He swept it into the drawer, holding down part of the mess inside so he could shove it closed. "You're still wrong."

"About what?" Exasperation sent her leaping up with enough force to knock the flimsy plastic chair to the ground. Ignoring the clattering, she paced the length of his desk, whacking her clipboard against her opposite palm. "The fact that the ordering system is woefully out of date? That the records department is a frightening black hole of misfiled bills and past–due invoices? That the scheduling for the brew process is haphazard? Or, perhaps I'm wrong about the whole fly–by–the–seat–of–your–pants attitude you have about everything here. But instead of listening to my ideas, you're submarining me at every opportunity."

He crossed his arms, making his biceps bulge. "I don't like change."

"Too bad. Change happens."

"Like *you* embrace it." Sarcasm reverberated in his deep bass.

"Of course I do, what do you call this?" She raised her clipboard like a shield.

"Change you control, not the kind some crazy new boss forces on you."

Natalie's eyes almost bugged out of her head and her chest heaved. "That is the dumbest things I have ever heard." Heat blazed in her cheeks.

Sean's blue eyes darkened and his eyelids drooped. "You burn hot."

Low and intense, his voice discombobulated her and had her clutching her clipboard to her chest.

"Hot?" She patted the sides of her French braid, tucking the loose strands behind her ears and straightened her glasses. "No. I am in firm control of my emotions."

At least she used to be. Then she met the insufferable Sean O'Dell, quite possibly the most annoying man on the planet. She should have known he was trouble when they they were introduced and he'd acknowledged her with a caveman grunt. But she'd been too distracted by his warm, mahogany–colored eyes, broad shoulders, and ruggedly handsome face half hidden behind a beard. His stinginess when it came to talking drove her nuts, and not just because he wasn't answering her questions, but because the gravel–edged timbre of his deep voice sent a delicious shiver down her spine every time he spoke. Knowing him, he probably spoke so infrequently to keep her off balance. He was as pleasant as ants at a picnic.

"Why don't you talk about this...stuff–" he pointed to her clipboard "–with your sister?"

Natalie almost looked around for a hidden video camera, because this had to be a prank. Unfortunately, there was no camera. She clutched her clipboard to her midsection so she wouldn't wring his neck. Sean wasn't dumb, but his purposeful thickheadedness was about to make her snap.

"Two very good reasons," she said, keeping her tone level, if laced with ire. "Number one, because Miranda got here nine days before I did and knows just as little about the history of this place as I do. Number two, because she's tied up with wedding plans."

He shrugged those broad shoulders, pulling his Sweet Salvation Brewery T–shirt tight across his muscular chest. "The changes will wait for her."

"The changes have been waiting for months. I'm done waiting." Her clipboard's edges bit into her palms. God, what was it about this man that made her crazy enough to want to wing her favorite accessory at him?

"Looks like we're at a standoff then, Sugar." He picked up the brochure from his desk and circled around to her side. One callused finger tipped the clipboard away from her chest, never touching her skin but close enough that his heat licked her. The air hummed around them. Hunger. Want. Need. All three zapped between them, and as strong as an electrical current on steroids. "Of course, if you were to scratch my back, I'd guarantee *your* needs were satisfied too."

Needs. Oh yes. She had them. Too damn many at the moment.

He slipped the brochure onto her clipboard. Fire ate its way up from her toes. The man had a death wish. It was the only thing she could come up with to explain why he kept purposefully pissing her off. "That's blackmail."

Sean chuckled, a sound that should never give her naked, naughty fun thoughts, but in his case did. "That's harsh, Sugar. It's negotiating, and if we do it right, we all walk away happy."

She wasn't falling for his brand of happy, no matter how tempting the messenger. "Forget it."

Instead of pushing him away, her words only brought him closer. His scent wrapped around her, teasing her senses and melting her resistance until the only thing grounding her to the real world was the clipboard in her hands.

He leaned in, his lips so close to hers that his words brushed against her skin. "You'll change your mind."

One inch. That's all it would take to close the distance between them. How very badly she wanted to eliminate the space was the only thing that kept her from doing it. So instead of jumping into the unknown abyss, she placed her palm over his fast–beating heart and stepped back. "What makes you so confident?"

He lifted her hand from his chest and kissed the center of her palm. Quick. Soft. Maddeningly effective. "Experience."

A knock sounded and she whipped her tingling palm from his grasp.

"What?" she and Sean barked at the same time.

Natalie spun around to face the door.

Billy stood there, his eyes round with surprise and more than a dash of fear. "The bottle delivery? Uh...it's not here."

"Call them," Sean said.

"I...uh...did." Billy's focus bounced from Natalie to Sean and back again. "They said the order had been canceled."

"By who?" Natalie asked. This was just the type of sloppy mistake that happened when things weren't organized.

Suddenly Billy became very interested in the toe of his tennis shoe. "Well...uh...you."

"I most certainly did not." And there was only one person at the brewery doing everything in his power to stall her every move.

Natalie spun on her heel and glowered at Sean.

Chapter Three

Natalie paced the eighteen strides from one end of Uncle Julian's large farmhouse kitchen to the other, annoyance eating away at her stomach lining like a dog with a rawhide bone. It had been two hours since she'd finally gotten the bottle delivery snafu straightened out and burned rubber on her way out of the Sweet Salvation Brewery parking lot, but she couldn't stop going over the confrontation with Sean. He was just...so...so...

She threw her hands up in the air. "Ugh!"

"You're going to wear a hole in the linoleum." Her sister Miranda took a bite of a peanut butter and honey sandwich.

The same sandwich Natalie had made and abandoned when she'd started telling her sister about her latest head–to–desk moment with the most stubborn man in the world. It was hard to express the righteous indignation of the unfairly wronged when her mouth was stuffed full of liquid–gold goodness.

She glanced down at the lime green and orange squares bright enough to hurt her eyes. "A hole wouldn't be the ugliest thing about this floor. We need to replace it anyway." She scrolled through her mental checklist for the house she and her sisters had inherited along with the brewery. "It's number three on the list of improvements we need to make to Uncle Julian's house."

Miranda snorted and took another bite. "Of course it is."

Her sisters had loved giving her shit for her lists ever since she'd drawn her first one in three shades of red crayons. Normally it didn't bother her, but today...Well, today everything bothered her. This was what happened when she didn't have a release. The lack of sex, her favorite stress reliever, was really starting to get to her.

Despite what her sisters thought, she wasn't a total prude. She just had always kept her personal life and her sex life separated. No fuss, no muss. But she was determined to end the separation and have a real relationship. Unfortunately, with all the hours she was putting in at the brewery, she hadn't gotten the chance to go out and find someone with the right combination of relationship potential and sex appeal.

"Don't start in on me, Miranda. I'm wound up enough as it is."

"No shit, you're as tight as a well–fed tick." Miranda gazed at her with her all–seeing eyes. "What happened to Miss Cool–Calm–and–Collected?"

"That *man*." She wound her fingers around her pearl necklace and twisted, her body primed with annoyance—and something more that started a warm, lazy southward wave from her lips to the juncture of her thighs. Damn, she needed to get laid.

Miranda shook her head, a teasing grin curling her lips. "Sean's great."

Oh yeah, great at driving her to distraction. "He's a pain in my ass."

"But he has a cute ass, something you used to appreciate in a man. Remember that hot football coach you introduced me to the last time I came to visit?"

Max. God, she really should have taken him up on that offer for goodbye sex.

Natalie started pacing again. Max hadn't ever made her lose her cool. She'd always been in control with him. Cool. Calm. Collected. Just like she'd always been, until Sean and his beard of mystery rocked her world.

She flopped down, landing with a thud on a chair next to her sister at the kitchen table. She swiped the half of the sandwich her older sister hadn't eaten yet and took a bite. "Why can't Sean just do what I want?"

"You mean like everyone else does?"

She shot Miranda a dirty look. "You don't. Neither does Olivia."

"We've built up a tolerance to your steamrolling ways."

Her spine stiffened. "I don't—"

"You're my little sister by a whole three minutes and I love you. But you can be a royal pain in the ass sometimes."

"Said with love, I'm sure," she grumbled. The truth of the statement stung more than she cared to admit.

"It is." Miranda reached over and covered Natalie's hand with her own. "You're a list maker and a plan maker. It's who you are. But not everyone is like that and you can't always control what other people do."

Sean's words echoed in her head loud enough that she couldn't help but repeat them. "Controlled change."

Miranda cocked her head, her eyes—the same sky–blue shade as Natalie's own—darkening with confusion. "Huh?"

Natalie shrugged off the almost–epiphany whispering from a dark corner of her mind. "Something *that man* said."

"He has a name."

She withdrew her fingers from her sister's grasp and crossed her arms over her belly. "He does."

"Say it." Damn, the stubborn set of Miranda's jaw meant trouble.

Normally, Natalie would have placated her or distracted her Type–A sister from the topic at hand. Wasn't that what every middle child's role in life was, especially when it came to their siblings? But for some reason, the situation with Sean tangled up her insides like a pair of earbuds languishing in a knotted mess at the bottom of her purse.

"Why should I?"

Miranda arched her perfectly waxed eyebrows and shrugged. "Because you're going to have to get him on your side if you want to make changes."

Her chest tightened at her sister's assertion. "We own the brewery. He's an employee."

"And in all the research you've done, you've discovered that making changes by fiat as opposed to getting your team on board is the most efficient way to do things?"

"Well, no." Natalie shifted in her seat and tried to quash the uncomfortable feeling of being wrong with the unmovable mountain of her stubbornness. "But I'm right."

"I'm not the one you need to convince." Miranda paused, sneaking a side–eyed glance at her sister. "Unless you just want to get rid of Sean."

"Fire him?" The question came out as a squeak and she ran her fingers across her necklace, counting sixteen pearls one way and then working her way back to her starting point. The old habit didn't help calm her. She'd made two revolutions in quick succession and her pulse hadn't slowed from all–hands–on–deck emergency mode.

"We do own the place." Miranda grabbed the chipped blue–stoneware plate and strode to the sink. "Of course, I never thought you were the kind to back away from showing someone the light. I didn't think convincing Sean would be that much of a challenge for you."

She fisted the necklace tight enough that the pearls made circular indentations in her palm. "It's not."

Miranda rinsed the plate and popped it in the ancient avocado–colored dishwasher before slamming it shut. "So untwist your pearls and make him a convert. It is the Sweet *Salvation* Brewery, after all. Aren't we all supposed to understand things better in Salvation?"

That had been Natalie's original intention when she'd pulled up stakes and moved back home. If she couldn't persuade Sean to see the light, what chance did she have of enlightening herself?

Working on about four hours of sleep thanks to the ever–present image of Natalie Sweet burned on the inside of his eyelids, Sean slouched against the wall in the Sweet Salvation Brewery break room in a nearly comatose state, waiting for the coffee to finish brewing.

The allure of closing his eyes and catching a few Zs tugged at him, but he knew as soon as he did, all he'd see was Natalie. The pearl necklace circling her throat, drawing attention to her soft, creamy skin. The ever–present cardigans that drove him nuts wondering what was hidden beneath. The tightly pulled–back hair and skeptical demeanor that fueled the resurgence of every librarian–inspired fantasy he'd never known he had.

Even after a night of tossing and turning, he could still feel the slight weight of her across his shoulder and the surprisingly muscular length of her thighs. Her sweet honeysuckle scent had stayed with him long into the night. For as tightly wrapped a package as she was, Natalie Sweet offered more temptation than the Playboy Mansion ever had.

And she was completely off limits.

The Sweet Salvation Brewery had saved him. He'd worked his way up from night cleaning crew to head brewmaster in a few years, and when he perfected the latest stout recipe, he'd solidify his position at the brewery with a blue ribbon win at the Southeast Brewers Invitational.

Julian Sweet had taken a chance on Sean despite him showing up as a man without a high school diploma, his real Social Security number, or the truth about who he was and where he'd come from. Sean sure as hell wasn't going to repay Julian by banging the dead man's niece as if she were a groupie who'd followed him into the bathroom at a movie premiere.

"Yo, Sean." Billy poked his head into the break room. "Some dude called for you."

He eyeballed the younger man. "Name?"

"Rupert Something–or–Other." He sauntered into the room, grabbed a coffee mug from the cabinet and rested a hip against the counter. "Talked too fast to get it all down. He said he'd call back."

Sean's gut clenched, sending his breakfast surging up the way it had gone down. He clamped his jaw shut and willed the bile into submission.

"What the hell kind of first name is Rupert anyway?" Billy asked.

The kind of name that brought back memories of dark closets with locked doors and warnings delivered with a backhanded swing.

The Styrofoam cup crumpled in Sean's grip. "Where was he calling from?"

He'd croaked out the question, but Billy didn't seem to notice. Instead the gangly, Southern version of a hipster grabbed the coffee pot and poured himself a cup of dark roast. "Sunny California."

The other side of the country. The black clouds of dread gathering around the edges of his vision cleared a bit before his gut twanged with suspicion. "How do you know he was in California?"

"Caller ID is a beautiful thing. If you ever talked to anyone on the phone, you would have realized that technology kicks ass. Damn man, you still use a pre–paid flip phone." Billy held out the coffee pot toward Sean before his gaze dropped to the crushed cup in Sean's fist. Shrugging, he slid the glass carafe back onto the warmer.

Sean had to play this close. If anyone at the brewery realized his name was Sean Duvin and not Sean O'Dell, there'd be more trouble than he ever wanted to deal with. The only thing worse would be if Rupert showed up on the brewery's doorstep with a camera crew and a mic.

Trying to maintain his facade of disinterest, he forced his fist to open and dropped the broken chunks of Styrofoam into the garbage. "And he asked for me?"

"Well, I thought it was a telemarketer, because it sure sounded like he'd said Sean Duvin or Darvin or Dugin instead of O'Dell, but I must have misheard because he got all chatty about how he hadn't seen you in years."

Almost ten, to be exact. Sean had walked off the stage, away from the cameras, and handed his bastard of a father his Oscar, saying he had to take a piss and promising he'd be right back. Instead, he'd stolen the first car he could hotwire and driven it as far as the gas in the tank would take him, shaved his head, traded in his tux for some Wrangler jeans, and hopped a Greyhound.

"Number?"

Billy dumped about a pound of sugar into his coffee cup. "Didn't leave one, but I wrote down the caller ID number." He pulled a crumbled piece of paper from the pocket of his worn jeans.

Sean held out his hand, and Billy slapped the torn corner of a fast food sandwich wrapper into his palm. One glance confirmed it was the number to the *Hollywood and Vine Reports* offices in Malibu. He'd seen the number enough in his formative years to know it by heart. If Rupert had stumbled onto his trail that meant his father wouldn't be far off, and if he never saw that bastard again in his life it would be too soon.

The blood in his veins turned to frozen sludge. "Message?"

"Nope."

That didn't mean Rupert didn't want anything. The sleazebag had spent most of the past decade writing about the "bright young talent who had disappeared off the face of the Earth." He wasn't about to stop now.

Sean yanked the brim of his Sweet Salvation Brewery baseball cap down with more force than was necessary. He needed space to figure out what—or more accurately, *where*—his next move was.

"And on less–happy news, the fermentation tank is leaking, but the fact that Natalie has spent the morning shut up in her office balances out that bit of bad news." Billy smirked at what he no doubt thought was a funny swipe at the boss. "You know, so she's not running around getting into everyone's business."

"Not funny." Sean glared at the skinny little twerp until he bounced nervously on his toes. "How bad's the leak?"

Billy shrugged. "Clyde's fussing with it, but it's gushing at a good clip."

The fermentation tank held more than twelve hundred gallons of not–yet–drinkable beer. If they couldn't fix the leak they'd lose nearly seven thousand bottles of beer. That would be the equivalent of using a flamethrower to light a cigarette in terms of damage to the brewery's bottom line. "Shit. Why didn't you tell me this first?"

Not bothering to stick around for the explanation, Sean marched out of the break room, took the first left and pushed through the swinging door leading from the offices to the brewery floor, where all the action took place.

Sean made a beeline toward the small crowd gathered around the stainless–steel tank with the cone–shaped bottom, the pointed end of which stopped a few feet off the brewery's cement floor. Clyde, the chief maintenance man, had folded himself nearly in two as he twisted his body to get a better look at the damage while avoiding the amber–colored geyser rushing out of the tank.

The whole mess got worse with each step Sean took. By the time the crowd parted for him, there was a river of beer surging out of the bottom of the fermentation tank. "Oh, fuck."

"You said it." Billy agreed.

Sean crouched down beside Clyde. The older man had enough lines on his forehead to double as a highway map, each one made even deeper with worry. That meant it was so bad it couldn't even be registered on a Richter scale.

"What's the verdict?" As if he needed to hear the words to know.

Clyde stood and every joint in his body cracked loudly in protestation as he straightened to his full height. Not one to be hurried by man or beer, he pulled a red bandana out of his back pocket and used it to dry his hands before folding it twice and stuffing it back home. "The fermenting beer is coming out of the bottom outlet hole."

"I see that." Sean managed, just barely, to keep the no–shit–Sherlock sarcasm out of his voice.

Clyde pointed a long, bony finger at the bottom of the tank. "That there bolt for the tri–clamp connection is shot."

The seriousness of the situation became crystal clear. "Which means the tri–clamp and the reducer connection are less than useless."

"Pretty much." The grizzled veteran of all the things that could go wrong at a brewery rocked back on his heels. "This," he pointed to the beer flowing down into the floor drainage trench, "is going to look like a drizzle before it's all said and done."

Sean followed the beer creek until his gaze hit the reference room. He looked longingly at the place where he had spent every night for the past few months trying to find just the right combination of yeast, hops, barley, and more for a stout beer to win the invitational. He wouldn't be locked behind that door anytime soon by the looks of the shitstorm in front of him.

He rubbed the back of his neck, hoping he could erase the niggling worry making his short hairs stand on end. They'd replaced the fermentation tanks not that long ago and adhered religiously to the maintenance schedule. "The tank is only a year old, how did this happen?"

"If'n I had to guess, I'd say someone either over–tightened the bolt or whacked it with something good and heavy."

Shock nailed Sean's feet to the concrete floor and for a minute all he could do was suck in air. "On purpose?"

Clyde quirked a fat gray eyebrow. "Lots of folks in town hold a grudge against the Sweets."

As if on cue, Natalie strode through the brewery's swinging doors. With her turquoise skirt, striped sweater, and the pearl necklace she was never without, she looked completely out of place among the staff with the T–shirts and stained jeans they wore.

If he'd thought his pulse was thumping before, he was a damn fool, because there were jet planes slower than his heart right now.

She pulled a pencil out of the messy bun thingy she'd twisted her light–brown hair into and started scrawling away on her clipboard without ever losing a step. The woman didn't strut. She didn't sway her hips. She didn't need to; he was already about to bust a nut as it was.

Clyde elbowed him in the ribs. "From what I hear, you're not much of a fan of a particular Sweet yourself."

"You shouldn't gossip." Sean averted his gaze and turned his body so he couldn't be tempted to peek at Natalie as she closed the distance between them in small, precise steps.

The old mechanic chuckled and clapped his palm against Sean's shoulder. "And you shouldn't give everyone so much to gossip about, with the way you avoid that woman like she's selling flea–infested puppies—but still look at her like she's a steak dinner and you're a staving man. When I was your age, a man knew how to make up his mind and act on it."

Sean wiped his palms on his jeans and focused on the fermentation tank that was leaking like a sieve. "I'll keep that in mind."

The hint of honeysuckle hit him a second before a clipboard appeared in his peripheral vision.

"Keep what in mind?" Natalie asked.

Sean sent up a quick prayer that, for once, the blunt–talking, take–no–prisoners Clyde wouldn't say exactly what was on his mind.

Chapter Four

The leak made no sense.

Natalie spritzed the purple orchid on her desk, one of the few splashes of color in her otherwise stark–white office. While Sean refused to review, let alone peruse, her efficiency plan for the brewery, he was borderline OCD on equipment maintenance—something she'd incorrectly assumed meant he'd be open to her reorganization ideas.

She stored the water bottle in the cabinet with a clear silicone liner on the shelf to catch any small drops that may escape and shut the door with a firm click.

Next up in her daily routine was a quick review of her color–coded calendar. She flicked the mouse to wake her laptop as she continued to turn the problem over in her mind. The fermentation tank had passed visual inspection two days before. She'd seen the documentation signed by Clyde to prove it. The man was territorial and doted on the brewery equipment like rich ladies spoiled their lapdogs. If the tank hadn't been up to par, he wouldn't have given it his seal of approval.

She needed data. Making a mental list of all the records she'd need, she pressed the intercom button on her phone to connect to Miranda's office. "Hey sis."

"Yeah?" Stress tightened Miranda's normally smooth voice.

The leak had everyone on edge. In the few months since the county council had voted down an effort to make alcohol manufacturing illegal in the county, the Sweet Salvation Brewery had pulled back from the financial abyss. But that didn't mean the brewery wouldn't take a hit from the thirty grand in lost revenue because of the leak. Miranda had the money end of things under control. What Natalie needed to focus on was finding and isolating the problem.

See a problem, fix a problem.

"Sorry to interrupt." Natalie smoothed back her hair that had started to fly away in her rush to get to the brewery floor earlier. "I need to get the maintenance, quality assurance, and accident documentation for the past three years."

"That sounds exciting. I take it you're on the case of the cursed fermentation tank?"

Ignoring her sister's sarcasm, Natalie nodded. "Exactly."

"Great. That means I can deal with the bars whose orders are being delayed." Miranda exhaled a frustrated sigh. "The folks at the Boot Scoot Boogie are pissed, and I need to go smooth some ruffled feathers."

The local country bar was their best client. They couldn't afford to lose the business. Not unless they wanted to part ways with a significant portion of staff.

"Let me grab those files from you before you head out." Natalie stood and took a step toward the door.

"I don't keep that stuff."

Please don't let them be in a file cabinet in the brewery's attic, AKA Spider World. "Who does?"

"Your favorite brewmaster."

Her feet froze to the oatmeal–colored area rug covering the pale gray cement floor. Enough goose bumps popped up on her arms to make them look like a topographical map of the Rocky Mountains.

Foreboding? Anticipation?

Not a question she felt like answering—even to herself.

The school of hard knocks had given Sean two important lessons before he'd graduated with honors. Number one: Something always goes wrong sooner than you expect. Number two: Bad news breeds faster than rabbits.

First a tabloid reporter on the phone and now the fermentation tank. Trouble had beaten a path to Salvation, and he had a sinking suspicion it wasn't about to leave anytime soon.

He scratched the scruff of his beard and contemplated the stacks of paperwork scattered across his desk before riffling through the closest tower. The maintenance reports were here somewhere. He let the crew have a lot of leeway on other parts of the brewery operations, but he didn't fuck around with people's safety. He'd learned a long time ago just how much being vulnerable and hurt messed with your head. He sure as hell wasn't going to put anyone else in that position.

He made it halfway through the pile before he wanted to kick his own ass for not using the damn filing cabinet that still had the price tag stuck to the top drawer. "Controlled chaos," he mumbled.

"Well, part of that's right." Natalie stood in his doorway.

Every strand of her light–brown hair was back in place, making him want to do nothing in the world so much as unclip it so he could watch it tumble down around her shoulders. Or was it longer? Would the ends curl around her nipples or brush her narrow waist? He'd been living like a damn monk for too long if the idea of seeing a woman's unbound hair made his mouth dry and his dick half hard.

Annoyed with his lack of control, he dropped a sheaf of papers onto his empty chair. "I don't have time for your billion–point plan right now."

"It's a twenty–five–point plan." Her chin shot up an inch. "And I'm not here for that. I'm looking for the maintenance, quality assurance, and accident reports."

He glanced around at his kamikaze, open–air filing system. "Welcome to the club."

"You don't have them?"

A hint of shame tinged his earlier self–recriminations, making his pulse pick up speed. Nothing like having to admit to your nemesis, even if it wasn't out loud, that you sucked. "They're here somewhere."

Her blue eyes went wide and her fingers twisted around the pearl necklace. "You don't have a filing system?"

Sean shrugged. "You're looking at it."

Her long fingers sailed over each round white pearl. Damn, he really wanted to know the story behind that necklace. He'd never seen her without it. The woman probably showered in it.

In half a breath, he had a fully realized vision of her soft, creamy, naked skin covered in suds. The mental image sucked all the air out of the room and turned his half chubby into a full–blown hard–on.

Natalie looked around at the paper explosion in his office. "How do you live like this?"

He kept one of the taller stacks of paper between them to block her view of the growing bulge behind his zipper. "Cleanliness is over rated."

"You're hilarious." She didn't even bother to look his way as she surveyed the damage. "Okay, if we divide the room up into equal portions, we should each be able to take a quadrant to search. Divide and conquer for the win."

He shifted from one leg to another. Spending time in close quarters with Natalie, watching her skirt swirl around her ass, wasn't going to help him lose this boner anytime soon. "Let me look. I'll let you know when I find them."

She tossed her clipboard onto his guest chair—the one spot in the whole office unencumbered by piles of paper. "We can get through this whole mess faster if we work together. I can even devise an organizational structure for the records based on your work habits."

Excitement turned her cheeks pink as she chewed her bottom lip and bounced from foot to foot. If she ever looked at him with the same amount of giddy anticipation, he'd be in even worse trouble than he was already.

"Trust me." She locked gazes with him, hitting him with the full force of her blue eyes. "People pay me big bucks to do that for them."

"Any other option?" He already knew the answer to that one.

She grinned. "You could toss me over your shoulder again and throw me in the cooler."

The idea of touching her held more appeal than it should. He took a half step forward.

Natalie jumped back, but not before he noticed her quick intake of breath and how her eyes darkened with what looked at lot like lust.

He winked, loving the fact that he'd knocked her by–the–book self off kilter. "Gotcha."

He couldn't wait to do it again.

The filing cabinet was empty. Not just empty, but the drawers were still taped shut and the receipt—dated three years ago—sat inside one of the drawers. There was at least an inch of undisturbed dust on the handle. Natalie glanced around Sean's paper–filled office. The man made less sense than wearing a ball gown to yoga class.

"Are you allergic to metal?"

He looked up from the stack of papers he was going though and peeked at her from beneath the brim of the hat he always wore. "Why?"

Spinning around to face him, she put her hands on her hips. "I'm trying to figure out why you'd leave a perfectly good four–drawer filing cabinet complete with hanging folders and color–coded tabs empty, and instead leave everything stacked a mile high on every flat surface."

He did that one–sided grin thing that made her stomach do the loop–de–loop. "I have a system."

"How's that working for you so far?"

Sean looked around as if seeing his office for the first time, taking in the towers that had given up the ghost and fallen long ago and the ones wobbling with any significant exhale of breath. "Pretty shitty."

Natalie chuckled at his assessment. Blunt. Honest. To the point. If he wasn't such a giant pain in her ass, she'd be in danger of falling for him. Lucky for her, she'd already created a list of attributes she wanted in a man, and Sean didn't qualify. Even if he had, he was her employee.

A heavy sigh escaped from her lips. Nothing to do but move on, so she took stock of the situation. They needed to make quick work of organizing the pounds of paperwork so she could take a look at the records and determine if there was any kind of a pattern to the things going wrong at the brewery. First the canceled bottle delivery that everyone at the brewery–including Sean– and now the suspicious leak. Then she'd be able to create a solution to avoid making the same errors in the future. Easy–peasy.

"Okay. Here's the plan. I'll start with the credenza. You tackle the desk. Make stacks for different types of paperwork. All quality assurance reports go in one stack, for example. Once you have your new piles, we'll transfer them to the filing cabinet. Pull out anything you see from the last three months and put those files on the guest chair."

He looked as though she'd just asked him to give a speech on national television while buck naked and doing one–armed pushups–an image that flashed into her mind and put her nether regions on full alert. Needing to do something with her suddenly jittery hands, she trailed her fingers across her cool, round pearls.

"I know it seems like a lot…" Her words came out in a breathy half whisper. "But I promise we'll be done before you know it."

She'd seen that pursed–lips look on Sean's face before. Her clients always doubted before they became true believers. "I won't even say the word flowchart while we're doing it."

"You just did." He crossed his arms, pulling his Sweet Salvation Brewery T–shirt tight across his broad shoulders and making the short sleeves hike up, showing off plenty of sinewy muscle, from his thick forearm to his bulging biceps.

Her mouth turned to sawdust and her mind to mush. "Did what?" Damn, that breathy sound again.

"Say flowchart." Sean took a step closer, not with intent, but as if he couldn't help himself.

In normal circumstances, a step here or there wouldn't make a bit of difference. But one stride on his long legs in the tiny, crowded office brought him almost toe to toe with her. Awareness crackled in the air between them, cool and crisp like the first burst of autumn after a decade's worth of summer humidity. Solid brawn was not on her potential partner attribute list. Neither were broad shoulders or a sharp wit that snapped at her funny bone when she least expected it.

Feeling like she'd been set adrift on a roiling ocean, she grabbed frantically for a lifeline. Bossiness always worked wonders. "You know, you're a real smartass. Enough stalling, let's get to work."

Something dark and hungry swirled in his brown–eyed gaze before it sank to her mouth. "It's always the chatty ones."

He was wrong. It was the quiet ones who were dangerous as hell, but she couldn't get the words out to correct him. She couldn't even move. Truth be told, she didn't want to put even a millimeter more space between them. The foot between them was too much already.

Wrong. It was so achingly wrong, but it felt so good in the short term that she didn't care. Which was exactly what had gotten her to the point in her life where she compartmentalized sex so much that fuck buddies had become a way of life. She'd relationship–blocked herself one time too many and she was done with it. But something about Sean was different. He wasn't like her past boyfriends, the ones she could steamroll right over and remold into her preferred type.

It took everything she had, but she took a step back, far enough that the metal filing cabinet handles jabbed her in the spine. The pain was a physical manifestation of the yowling protest deep in her core.

Sometimes fixing a problem hurt like a bitch.

As if waking from a hypnotic state, Sean shook his head. He took off his hat and ran his hand through his thick, wavy, jaw–length hair, revealing a three–inch jagged scar. At that angle, with the light hitting him just right, a memory struggled to break through the haze. Something familiar and yet unknown tugged at her subconscious.

"What?"

An electric spark danced up her arm, setting off a chain–reaction tingle that put a little loosey–goosey in her step. "You remind me of someone."

He jerked the hat back on and hunched his shoulders. "Who's that?"

"I don't know, but it'll come to me."

He shoved the hat back on and pulled the brim low. "Must have one of those faces."

"No, it's more than that." A picture formed in her mind. A man. A porch swing. A bunch of daisies. Damn, it was so clear and yet so fuzzy. "It's right on the edge of my brain, like when something's right on the tip of your tongue but you can't remember it for the life of you."

He grunted.

She opened her mouth to tease him for his normal noncommittal response—

But the emergency siren blared in the hall and she nearly jumped out of her skin.

Chapter Five

Sean was out the door before his brain had finished processing the blaring alert loud enough to wake the dead three states away. Natalie matched him step for step as he booked it down the narrow hallway toward the swinging brewery doors.

In a brewery, things could get Chewbacca hairy in a heartbeat.

For example, a guy in Maryland had passed out while driving his forklift in the cooler because the area hadn't been properly ventilated and the carbon monoxide emitted from the forklift got to him. He wasn't discovered in time and ended up dying from carbon monoxide poisoning. And a man in California had lost several fingers when they got caught in the metal shaft of the conveyor system. Bottling machines across the country had maimed dozens of brewery employees.

They'd already dealt with the fermentation valve malfunctioning this morning. He hated to even imagine what unholy hell awaited him on the other side of the brewery doors.

No one would set the emergency alarm off just for shits and giggles.

He paused, his palm flat against the wood, his protective instincts rushing to the forefront. "Wait in the office."

Natalie angled her chin up, showing just how ready she was for a fight. "Why?"

Realization, armed with flashy brass knuckles, gave him a quick one–two to the jaw.

Because it matters if she gets hurt. Not that it didn't with anyone else at the brewery, but...Sean shoved whatever thought came next into a deep hole.

"Just do it." He pushed the door open and walked straight into the all–encompassing arms of total fucking chaos.

In the middle of the brewery floor, three guys were wrestling an out–of–control hose the size of a fireman's water hose that was flying around like a python on steroids. The hose twisted and turned, cutting off access to the shutoff valve that controlled it. But water wasn't spraying out of the nozzle, so what in the hell was making it do that? One of the men, Mike, dove for the hose and flattened it.

"Turn the hose off," Sean hollered.

"We already did, the valve won't shut off," Mike said.

He started to sprint toward the commotion when someone grabbed his T–shirt and yanked him backwards.

"Watch out!" Natalie yelled over the uproar on the brewery floor.

Two women whizzed past him in a blur.

Hailey had abandoned her post in the front office. Armed with a high stack of towels, she hightailed it over to a crowd gathered by the fermentation tank spill. Epie followed in her footsteps with the oversized first–aid kit. Blood splattered her white brewery T–shirt.

Billy sat at the center of the circle of people on the other side of the room, bleeding like crazy from a small cut on his forehead but still talking a mile a minute.

"Fuck." His fingers locked around Natalie's wrist, halting her in mid–stride as she attempted to follow the women. "It may not be safe."

"I'll take the chance." She yanked free and hustled after the two women.

The hose broke free from Mike's grasp, clipping him in the head as it flew into the air. Blood rained down the foreman's face and he crumpled into the fetal position, clutching his head.

The other two men ran to his aid while the hose clanged its metal nozzle against the concrete floor.

Sean bolted across the open space, his gaze locked on the hose whipping back and forth. He paused outside of its vicious reach. He had to time it just right. One wrong move and he'd be bleeding as bad as Mike—and that was his optimistic assessment. It could be worse. One guy he'd heard about in California got clipped in the head with a hose fired up with carbon dioxide instead of water and had ended up in the hospital for five days, three of which he had no idea who or where he was.

Carbon dioxide.

Fuck.

Odorless. Tasteless. Fatal at high doses. The Sweet Salvation Brewery used the carbon dioxide produced during the fermentation process to purge the beer bottles of air prior to filling, and to protect the beer from getting a funky oxidation taste. If carbon dioxide was building up inside the brewery, everyone was in danger, not just those close enough to get whacked by the out–of–control hose.

He leaped forward and wrapped his hands around the thick hose near the nozzle—a real nasty piece of business made up of metal and bad intentions. It bucked against him as if it were alive and pissed off. Beads of sweat popped out along his hairline and snaked their way down his neck. His muscles strained with the effort of keeping the hose flattened down. His grip slipped a fraction and the hose reared up, coming within an inch of his head. Close enough he could hear the high whine of gas streaming out.

Straining with effort, he clamped down tight on the hose and pushed it to the concrete floor hard enough that the nozzle clanged in protest. He straddled the line and leaned all his weight forward into his arms.

"Turn off the valve!" he yelled, his attention never wavering from the beast in his grasp.

"It's already off," someone hollered back.

Sean shook his head. "Turn off the carbon dioxide valve."

Feet pounded the floor behind him.

A second later the squeak of the valve sounded.

The hose slackened.

Relief slackened the tension in his muscles and his arms went limp. He rocked back to his heels and stood before pivoting to take stock of his crew.

On automatic pilot, his gaze found Natalie. She was pressing a fast–reddening towel to Mike's forehead. Sean's gut tightened, but he continued to scope out the situation. The rest of the crowd by the fermentation tank looked as if they'd just finished running a marathon with zombies hot on their heels, but other than Billy and Mike, everyone was unharmed. At least for now. They'd all suffer if they didn't get some fresh air in to dilute the carbon dioxide thickening the air.

"Open the bay doors," he yelled.

One of the younger crew members sprinted over and pulled the heavy chains that raised the metal doors, letting in a blast of cold air.

Hailey, her face pinched and pale, stepped into his line of vision.

"Damage report," he snapped.

The unflappable office manager, didn't even blink at his sharp tone. "Ambulance is on the way. Billy's head is bleeding like crazy and he's going to need stitches is my guess, but he's still cracking jokes. Mike should go in the ambulance with him. He'll probably need stitches too."

Sean nodded. "Everyone else is okay?"

She shrugged. "A little freaked out, but good."

Relief loosened the iron grip squeezing his shoulders tight. Still, he needed to confirm Hailey's report with his own eyes. He hustled over to Mike and crouched down, close enough that Natalie's honeysuckle scent twisted around him, calming his jumpy nerves.

"How you doing, man?"

"I'll live." Mike's grin, though strained, was genuine. "If I had to get hit somewhere, the head was probably the spot to take the beating."

Sean patted him on the shoulder and glanced at Natalie, who was running her fingers up and down that necklace as though they were prayer beads. "You okay?"

She nodded, not even a single strand of light-brown hair daring to shake free from her bun. "Fine, but I need to talk to you."

Hailey took over as Mike's temporary nurse and Natalie walked Sean over to the shut-off valves. He bent down and double checked that both were completely closed. Masking tape labels were stuck to the front of each valve, and water was clearly written across one in big bold lettering, CO_2 across the other.

Worry itched its way up his spine. His trouble detector had been honed to a fine point by spending his formative years under the control of a man faster with his backhand than a Ferrari could get to sixty miles per hour.

"Look." She pointed to the masking tape labels. "Somebody added these."

He peered closer. He didn't recognize the handwriting, but that didn't mean shit. Of course, that didn't stop the hair on his forearms from standing at attention. "How can you tell?"

"Check this out." She peeled back one corner of the tape, revealing a water drop etched into the valve handle. "That's not a mistake."

Sean pinched the bridge of his nose hard enough to make him almost sneeze. "Agreed."

"So what are we going to do about it?" Natalie asked.

Sean watched Deputy Epson walk to the middle of the brewery floor and take a long, quizzical look at the fermenting tank that stood about twelve feet high. With careful steps he circled the tank, careful to avoid the beer pooled on the floor and the blood droplets from Mike's and Billy's injuries, all the while tapping his department–issued hat against the flat of his fleshy palm.

The soft *thwap, thwap, thwap* sound was starting to reverberate in Sean's head like the thunder of a fast–approaching summer storm. It was no secret that the Sweet family and local law enforcement had a long and colorful relationship that encompassed everything from nude protests on the courthouse lawn to running moonshine in the old days.

He crossed his fingers behind his back, an old but comforting gesture. Judging by the way Natalie practically hummed with nervous energy beside him, he wasn't the only one waiting for the other shoe to drop.

"Walk me through this whole thing again." Deputy Epson settled his brown hat back on his freckled bald head. "Start from the beginning."

Natalie groaned beside him. They'd already told the story three times, and her tone had turned from annoyed to glacial by the third telling. The fourth might make her snap, which was the last thing she or the brewery needed right now.

He placed his hand on the small of her back to warn and reassure her. She slid a sideways look his way, but her muscles relaxed under his touch. He wished he could say the same. Just the little bit of contact, buffered by her softer–than–soft sweater, jangled up his arm and expanded in his chest like a hot air balloon, filling him up and making him empty at the same time.

Unsettled and annoyed, he jerked his hand away and shoved it into his jeans pocket. "Billy was cleaning a beer spill."

Natalie cleared her throat and trailed her fingers across the line of pearls circling her delicate throat. "Because the fermentation valve malfunctioned for reasons we've yet to determine, but I'm telling you now I'm pretty suspicious about it."

Epson's face remained stubbornly neutral and he kept quiet despite the pause in the conversation. The deputy might think he had the silent treatment's intimidation factor down pat, but he failed to deliver the underlying current of aggression that had always made Sean's dad's quiet explosions so much more deadly.

"Billy hooked up the hose to that line there to clean up the beer mess on the floor after we got the formation tank leak contained." Sean pointed to where the three–inch brass fitting was screwed onto the line labeled water.

Natalie squatted down by the valves and ran her long fingers across one knob. "But if you look closely, you'll see someone swapped the labels on the water valve and the carbon dioxide valve." She flicked the edge of the masking tape and pulled it back an inch to reveal the water droplet etched into the metal behind the handmade carbon dioxide label. "He hooked up to a carbon dioxide line instead of the water line. The pressure ripped the hose from his hands and the nozzle caught him right between the eyes."

Epson scribbled in his notebook. "And another man was injured?"

Sean nodded and glanced at the clock above the deputy's head. "Mike got clipped by the hose too." Both he and Billy were at the Salvation County Medical Complex. Hailey had promised to call as soon as the docs got done with them.

"What makes you think this is foul play as opposed to..." The deputy paused and pursed his lips, as if trying to think of an appropriate way to phrase the rest of his question. "A sloppy operation?"

First Natalie and her flowcharts, and now this. Did everyone think he ran a shoddy shop? Sean clenched his jaw tight enough to crack his first molar. Tension throbbed in his shoulders and the corded muscle in his neck twanged like a banjo in a speed–playing match.

"It's part of a pattern." Natalie clamored to his defense—or at least the Sweet Salvation Brewery's defense. "We've had dropped deliveries, the fermentation tank leak, and now this."

Epson quirked an eyebrow. "You have internal reports on any of these problems?"

Sean slid his gaze toward Natalie, whose face had gone from pale to pink to cherry in about three heartbeats. "We're working on gathering that now."

"No problem." The deputy took three steps toward the door leading to the offices. "Let me see what you've got so far."

Sean pictured the papers flooding every available flat surface in his office and wanted to kick himself in the ass for letting it get that bad. "We can't."

The deputy's eyes narrowed suspiciously. "Why not?"

"We were in the middle or an organizational overhaul when all this started happening, and our files are in a bit of disarray right now." Natalie's normally honey–smooth voice came out twisted and strained.

"That seems to be the case for a lot of things around here," the deputy deadpanned. "You folks keep in touch, let me know if anything else happens." Epson slid his notebook into his shirtfront pocket and sauntered over to the door.

Sean watched the deputy disappear through the swinging doors, knowing that despite the circumstantial evidence, the local sheriff's office wasn't going to expend many man hours over a problem at the brewery run by the most disliked family in Salvation. The Sweets weren't exactly pariahs anymore, but that didn't mean the townsfolk welcomed them.

Natalie crossed her arms and gave him a hard stare. Without her seemingly ever–present clipboard, the move squeezed her tits together until the top button on her fuzzy cardigan looked like it was about to wave the white flag. His dick twitched behind his zipper.

Yeah, he was a real bastard for checking her cleavage out at a moment like this, but he was also a man who'd become a little too intimately acquainted with his right hand lately.

"My face is up here, Sean."

Natalie's declaration blasted him back to the here and now.

Busted. Smooth move, dude.

Heat throbbed in his cheeks, but he managed to raise his gaze to her icy blue eyes. "We're going to have to find the bastard on our own."

She nodded. "Agreed, but we need to make a plan."

"Come by my house tonight."

"Why your house? Why not here, now?"

He glanced over his shoulder at the commotion picking back up on the brewery floor. "Because we don't know who's listening."

She looked around at the staff members getting back to work. No matter what might happen, she had to know the beer wouldn't wait, a fact even the most nervous of workers knew. "Point taken."

"Come by after work." Feeling like he'd just made a deal with the sexiest devil there was, Sean jammed his hat lower over the last scar his dad ever gave him and followed the deputy's path out the door.

Chapter Six

Four hours and sixteen minutes later, Natalie rested her cheek against her desk's cool laminate and felt her eyelids flutter shut. The chill soaked into her overheated flesh. Her sigh of relief was as heartfelt as that of a sorority girl nuzzling up to the porcelain god during rush week.

She could handle problems of the organizational kind without getting a single hair out of place. But when it came to probable sabotage and the prospect of being at Sean's house tonight, her insides turned all wibbly–wobbly.

Growing up as the quiet, contained one in the wild bunch known as the Sweets of Salvation, she'd always been snowed under by her family's brashness and crazy ways. Every time she'd gone with her sisters to bail her parents out of jail for one crazy protest or another against the powers that be, anxiety had tightened her entire body until the darkness threatened to eat away at her vision. All of that culminated in Natalie not being able to leave her college dorm room for two weeks until Dr. Kenning had given her the tools to deal with the overwhelming thing called life. So it made sense that all the goings–on at the brewery had her on edge.

Worry that there would be more mishaps accounted for seventy–nine–point–three percent of the discombobulated mess swirling around her. She attributed a solid twenty–point–seven percent to the man who expressed himself through grunts, clipped sentences, and strong muscles that made her weak in the knees.

"You don't look so hot, sis." Miranda's tone broke down into one part exhaustion and two parts concern.

Natalie snapped into a sitting position and slid her hands across her hair, ensuring every strand was in its proper spot, then patted her flushed cheeks.

"I feel plenty hot." And bothered. Too much time had passed since she'd had sex and relieved all the stress build up. Way. Too. Damn. Long.

"Will it make you feel better to know that I completed the safety check on the brewery while you were talking to the ever–helpful law enforcement officer?" Miranda asked, rolling her eyes when she mentioned Deputy Epson.

"He's just doing his job."

Her sister held up a piece of paper. "You haven't seen what the sheriff's office just e–mailed me."

It had only been a few hours. This didn't bode well. Natalie fought the urge to let her shoulders slump in defeat. "God, what now?"

"A police report that says, and I quote—" Miranda cracked the piece of paper dramatically "—'Not suspicious in nature, but most likely due to slipshod maintenance'."

"Don't let Clyde hear that, his head would pop right off." Natalie gave in and sank back into her chair. Well, as much as she could with the extra–firm lumbar support cushion. Was a little let–bygones–be–bygones too much to ask for in Salvation? Apparently so.

Her landline rang and the dread slithered straight down her spine. She really needed to chill out. It wasn't like the receiver was going to explode a la *Mission Impossible* as soon as she picked it up.

Hopefully.

She pressed the speaker button. "Sweet Salvation Brewery, Natalie Sweet speaking."

"Holy shit, what is going on down there?" The familiar voice of the youngest Sweet triplet, Olivia, made Natalie smile despite everything. "Ruby Sue Jepson said all hell's breaking loose at the brewery."

"What are you doing talking to Ruby Sue?" Miranda asked, moving closer to the desk so she didn't have to shout the question.

"Begging for some of her pecan pie."

"You need comfort food enough to call and try to pry that recipe from the woman who's sworn to take it to her grave?" Natalie's hand shot to her pearl necklace, each warm orb a reminder of the advice Dr. Kenning had given her about accepting that there are some things you can change and some you can't—the ultimate frustration of every control freak in the world. "Forget the brewery, what's going on in your world?"

"Nice try, sis, but I won't be distracted." Olivia laughed. "Fess up. Now."

Miranda sat down on Natalie's chair, nudging her sister aside so they each had a butt cheek on the white leather seat. “We’ve had some problems,” Miranda said.

“You call five people going to the hospital ‘some problems’?” Olivia’s voice crackled through the speakerphone.

“It was only two,” Natalie responded. “And that was two too many even if the paramedics said the wounds were minor.”

“What happened?”

Natalie glanced at Miranda, who gave her a go–ahead shrug. “One of the guys was cleaning up the fermentation leak and connected a hose to the carbon dioxide valve instead of the water valve. The end result was two guys down after getting hit in the head with the hose.”

“Why do I have the feeling there’s more to this?” Olivia asked.

“Because there is.” Natalie surprised herself with the harsh certainty in her voice. “The valves were mislabeled.”

“Sloppy work?”

Miranda shook her head, as if Olivia could see her over the phone line. “We don’t think so.”

“Keep going,” Olivia drawled.

Natalie unfurled her pointer finger. “We’ve had deliveries get canceled when they shouldn’t be.” Her middle finger went up. “The fermentation tank leaked because someone tightened the bolt too much or whacked it.” A third upraised finger joined the other two. “Then the hose accident that sent Billy and Mike to the hospital.”

“So who’s got a hard–on for the Sweet Salvation Brewery’s failure?” Olivia asked.

"Not as many people as when Miranda first got here," Natalie quipped. "But they're still out there."

"I wish I was there to help." Something more than sisterly solidarity leant a bitterness to Olivia's wistful tone.

Twins weren't the only ones with that whole otherworldly–connection thing, and Natalie's triplet alert was letting off a low–level vibration in the back of her head. Flighty and dramatic since birth, Olivia was the wild child of the three. The true Sweet who had never given a damn about what others thought—at least that was the image she projected. Still, something was off, Natalie was sure of it.

Wishing she was better at the touchy–feely stuff, she tried to figure out what to say to get Olivia to open up, but before she could, Miranda leaned in close to the phone's speaker.

"You know we love you," her sister said. "But there's not much more that can be done than what we're already doing."

"Still..."

"Forget it, Olive Breath," Miranda said, smiling as she used their baby sister's most–hated nickname. "You just started a new job that doesn't involve swimsuits in January while wearing feet–destroying stilettos. We'll see you in two months for your vacation."

Olivia giggled, the familiar sound silencing the warning bells in Natalie's head. "Man, some days I wish I was still modeling. Taking off to come see you two whenever I wanted was so much easier."

"Two words to reinforce your decision to retire from the runway: pecan pie." Natalie's stomach rumbled as soon as she spoke the words.

"Excellent point," Olivia said in mock seriousness. "And now I'm hungry again. I don't suppose I could get either of you to overnight me a pie from The Kitchen Sink."

"Forget it." The realization that she'd skipped lunch made Natalie's stomach fold in on itself in agony. "If I make it down to the diner today, I'm eating all the pecan pie Ruby Sue has myself."

"So much for sisterly love."

She rubbed her abdomen. "Exactly."

"So Natalie," Olivia said. "If the cops are a no–go, have you figured out a plan yet, or are you wearing the pearls down to nothing?"

Natalie clasped her hands in her lap and raised her chin. "I'm going to figure out who did it."

"That's it? No flowchart? No sixty–six point plan?" Olivia teased.

"I'm not without street smarts," Natalie shot back. The silence from her sisters that followed her pronouncement spoke volumes. "Anyway, Sean is helping."

A plotting gleam lit Miranda's eyes. "The, and I quote, 'monosyllabic Neanderthal', end quote, who is the most annoying man in the world?"

"Oh, I like him already," Olivia said. "Tell me more." Natalie could just imagine Olivia's face taking on a devious shine at the mention of a boy. Some things never changed. "Is he cute?"

She locked her hands together so tightly that she nearly lost circulation in her right hand. "That's not important."

"Damn, I practically see the blush over the phone line," Olivia teased. "He's that hot, huh?"

"Oh shut up." Natalie flipped the bird at the phone.

"Stop stirring up trouble." Miranda stood up and walked to the door.

"Very funny." Natalie toyed with her pearls. As if she could get any more stirred up than she already was. She straightened an already neat stack of folders on her desk.

Olivia let loose with a wolf whistle. "That all sounds like code for office nookie."

Natalie's hand slipped and she knocked one of the folders to the floor. The contents spilled out like a waterfall.

"No!" She rolled out her chair too fast and one wheel went off her plastic mat, lodging the chair in place. "We are simply meeting at his house."

"*That* location is definitely more private," Miranda said, amusement turning up her mouth.

Natalie shoved against her desk with more force than necessary, freeing her chair and rolling herself halfway across the office in the process. "We're just talking business."

"At his house," Olivia teased.

"Yes." Natalie got up from her chair and walked over to where the folder had fallen.

"At his house?" Miranda asked.

God, they were like the Greek chorus standing just offstage with no purpose other than to bust her chops and remind her of where her own thoughts had been drifting ever since Sean had proposed meeting.

"Yes." She swept the papers back into the folder, not even bothering to ensure they were properly arranged, and shoved it back onto her desk.

"At his house." This time her sisters said it together, as in sync as if they stood shoulder to shoulder instead of on opposite coasts.

Natalie inhaled a deep breath. "Repeating the location won't change the fact that that it's only a business meeting." She yanked open her middle drawer and pulled a Tums bottle from her alphabetically arranged first–aid supplies.

"Uh–huh." Miranda nodded her head in mock seriousness. "A, ahem, business meeting with the hot brewmaster at his house, after hours, alone. Yep, that totally sounds on the up and up. Maybe I should call Ruby Sue and see what she thinks?"

Natalie almost dropped the bottle of Tums as she was shaking out the prescribed two tablets into her palm. The town of Salvation loved nothing more than to flap their gums about the Sweet family. It had been that way since the dawn of time, but she'd never been at the center of it. She'd been too quiet and boring for that.

"We're just giving you shit." Miranda hurried over, wrapped an arm around her shoulder and gave it a quick squeeze. "Don't worry. Your secret's safe with us."

"It's not a secret." Natalie relaxed against her sister. "It's just a business meeting."

She ignored the fizzy feeling in her stomach and the extra lightness in her lungs because it was just a business meeting. She popped the Tums in her mouth.

Really. That's all it was.

With Hailey, Natalie had finally found a kindred soul in the world of organization. Flicking her fingers across the color–coded and alphabetized personnel files in the brewery office manager's vanilla–scented front office, the staccato beating of her heart had smoothed out to a steady rhythm. Her vision lost the blurry haze around the edges and her shoulders inched their way down from her earlobes.

This morning's events had been a close call in more ways than one.

The files she'd pulled shook in her hands.

"Here, let me take those before you send everything flying." Hailey swept the files from Natalie's grasp and set them down on her desk. "Now you've got files for everyone who's been fired—that's the red tab—or quit—that's the blue tab—in the last year."

Pulling herself back to the present, Natalie ran through her mental checklist. "What about anyone who's been written up or suspended?"

"Green tab." Hailey pulled open a filing cabinet drawer without even having to look first. "Only one of those." She grabbed a thick folder and handed it to Natalie.

Someone had written the name at the top of the file in precise block letters: Sean O'Dell.

Natalie blinked rapidly in surprise. She looked up at Hailey's determinedly blank face. "Really?"

"Oh yeah." Hailey snorted jeeringly. "He and the last brewmaster had their moments."

Carl Brennan, the old brewmaster, was a real piece of work. He'd been so pissed off when Uncle Julian left the brewery to her and her sisters that he'd tried to run Miranda off the road after she'd fired him. The fact that Natalie hadn't thought of him already as being the possible cause for the breweries troubles just went to show how out of her element she was. "Is he still in jail or has he made bail?"

Hailey nodded. "Yep, the judge wasn't messing around when she set his bail and his family doesn't have that kind of money."

Natalie's stomach sank. So much for her number one suspect. "Family?"

"Yep, his wife, Joni, is a stylist down at Pig Tails Salon."

A pissed–off spouse who had knowledge of the brewery's workings? That sounded like a possible suspect to her. "Did Joni ever work at the brewery?"

"Nah, she came to visit every once in a while, but she's a teetotaler." Hailey's narrow shoulders shuddered. "How she manages that, I have no idea. If I was married to that man, I'd be using whiskey instead of milk in my cornflakes every morning."

"Thanks, Hailey." Natalie gathered her stack of personnel files and headed out the door.

An hour later, her vision blurry from going through so many files in her office, she glanced up at the clock. Five–fifteen. At this time of year, dusk was giving up its foothold on the horizon to full dark, and judging by the lack of chatter filtering in through her open door, most of the crew had left already.

Miranda had hit the road with her fiancée, Logan, a half hour ago to go check out wedding reception venues. They'd picked April Fool's Day for their wedding date—a testament to the Sweet family's reputation in Salvation.

Normally, Natalie was pulling out of the parking lot by 5:05, but Sean's file alone had taken her a half–hour to read through. Unlike the others, that file was a mess. Hiring documents were out of order and half filled out. The W–2 was missing. There wasn't much in it at all if she didn't count the many warnings written by Carl with the word "overturned" in her Uncle Julian's cramped scrawl at the top of the page.

Glancing down at Sean's contact sheet, she memorized his address and then closed the manila folder, the sound amplified by the silence around her. Her pulse revved inside her like a race car waiting for the green light. Of course she wasn't alone. Hailey didn't usually leave until after six. Same with Clyde, who was determined to fix the fermentation tank tonight. Still, she knew Sean was gone, and despite the fact that she shouldn't feel better when he was around—she did. Somehow he'd moved into a spot that she hadn't realized was empty and filled it perfectly.

With deliberate care, she ran her fingers across the pearl necklace's smooth orbs, closed her eyes and breathed in a calming breath.

After three ten–second inhales and exhales, she opened her eyes.

Ignoring the apprehension buzzing quietly in her mind, she opened the desk's bottom drawer and retrieved her purse. Crossing to the door, she made an extra effort to maintain her normal pace, and not one footstep faster.

She wouldn't fall prey to old habits. The amped–up breathing. The jittering that shook her inside and out. The tightness in her chest, squeezing her heart nearly in two. It had been too long, and she'd been doing so well.

Stop acting so silly.

Everything's fine.

However, as she strode down the hall, keeping a tight grip on her purse's shoulder strap, the anxiety remained. It was weak and muffled, like a bee trapped under a glass dome, but still it fluttered in the pit of her stomach. It was only a quick five-minute drive to Sean's house. All she had to do was get there.

Chapter Seven

The smell of burnt popcorn overwhelmed every cubic inch of air in Sean's kitchen and living room. While his converted firehouse home was drafty enough that a continuous breeze swept across the exposed brick walls and over the hardwood floors, it was no match for the stench.

"Great," he muttered to himself as he threw open the window over the sink.

The night's chill rushed in, freezing the hairs inside his nose, and he shoved the window closed again. As soon as he did, the stink hit him square in the face. He was weighing the benefits of freezing versus being a mouth–breather when the doorbell dinged.

He whipped around and stared at the front door. *She* probably never burned popcorn. Hell, she probably hand–popped her own organic kernels in something vintage for the prescribed five–point–two minutes.

Diiiiiiiiing!

Longer this time. As though she knew he was inside trying to stuff the last pair of dirty Jockey shorts under the bed. In reality, he'd rolled all the clothes from his floor into a ball and crammed them into the dryer fifteen minutes ago. God, he was pathetic. It was as if his life had turned into a chick flick and he was the permanently friend–zoned, no–nuts whiner character.

Well, he hadn't played that kind of guy when he was in Hollywood, and he sure wasn't going to start now. Pulling his head out of his ass, he marched over to the front door and yanked it open.

Natalie stood shivering in the soft glow of his front porch light, hopping from foot to foot. "Thank God, I thought you were ditching me again."

"Nope." He stepped back so she could enter, feeling suddenly warmer despite the cold wind following her inside.

"Wow. This is not what I expected." She completed a full circle in the middle of his great room. "Not at all."

Sean looked around the converted firehouse, with its cavernous great room that flowed into the kitchen without any interior walls, and all he saw was work. He'd painstakingly finished the hardwood floors and filled in the brick's mortar where time had chipped it away, but his mental to–do list went on for several pages.

She brushed her palm across the uneven, exposed brick walls. "These are awesome."

Having seen her pristine, white, dirt–never–stood–a–chance office, he had a hard time believing the unfinished, raw house did anything other than give her the heebie–jeebies. "They're the original firehouse walls. Same with the metal staircase that goes up to the loft."

"But not the floors," she mused.

Sean looked down at the still shiny hardwood floors. Each board represented the best money he'd ever spent on therapy—also the only money he'd ever spent on therapy. "I added them. It was just concrete before."

"It's beautiful." She turned on the full force of her brighter–than–a–Klieg–stage–light smile. "But it's missing something."

"An air freshener," he quipped.

"Nothing kills burned popcorn smell but time. I know that from personal experience." She laughed. "No, you're missing a fireman's pole. This was the old East County Firehouse, right?"

"Yeah, Ruby Sue bought it at auction. I'm renting it from her. It never had a pole."

"That's too bad, I would have loved to have given it a try."

Just the mental picture of Natalie sliding down the pole with her skirt flying up was enough material to fill the spank bank for a decade.

He clenched his jaw so tightly it made his temples ache. *Down, boy. She's your boss. The one who wants to change everything about the brewery. Plus she doesn't even like you, let alone want to sleep with you.*

His stubborn dick ignored the advice as he stood by the closed front door and watched her stroll around the open space, looking as if she fit right in.

Stopping next to the big–screen TV he never turned on, she shrugged off her puffy winter coat, revealing a pale–blue cardigan with a row of tiny buttons sparkling in the light. Sean jammed his hands into his jeans pockets to keep from reaching out for her.

He'd never understood the naughty librarian thing some guys had—not until he met Natalie Sweet.

All he wanted to do was unwrap her.

Still scoping out the space, she laid her coat over the back of his slate-gray couch, put her hands on her hips, and inhaled a deep breath. The move stretched her soft cardigan enough that her buttons deserved hazard-duty pay.

And he thought he'd been hard before. There were forests with less wood than he sported in his jeans right now.

"I don't want to freak you out, but I have paperwork for you." She nodded toward her tan leather satchel she'd set on the floor. "But let's talk about what's going on at the brewery first."

Everything hard behind his zipper started to deflate. Nothing like a little bad-news reality to get rid of a raging hard-on. Someone with insider-level knowledge of the Sweet Salvation Brewery was behind the trouble. He knew it like he knew the smell of fresh hops.

"I need a beer for this." He rubbed his forehead. "Want one?" He crossed the open great room to the kitchen and opened the fridge.

"Sure, thanks."

He reached past the recently released Sweet Proposal Ale and grabbed two unlabeled, brown long-neck bottles. Watching Natalie unpack a notebook and three pens from her bag, he popped the caps and strolled over to the couch.

He set the bottles on the refurbished pallet coffee table next to her stuff. "Something I'm working on."

"For the brewers invitational?" She picked it up and took a long, slow drink. Her eyes closed and she savored the dark brew.

Sean's mouth went dry and he sat down beside her. "Yep. A stout."

"This is good." She held up the bottle in a toast.

"But not great." He'd been working on the recipe for months. The dark stout's flavoring emphasized the slightly sour notes produced by the dry–roasted malt and burnt–caramel bitterness, but it was missing something. What that thing was, he didn't have a fucking clue.

Natalie took a second swig and then her pink tongue darted out to capture a dot of creamy foam from her lip. "I don't know, I might argue with you on that point."

He couldn't look away from her full lips and imagining how they'd taste. "You argue about everything."

"Only when I'm right." She winked playfully and twisted on the couch to face him, bringing her knee in contact with his.

Heat, tension, and something he didn't want to define strung his body tight. "You ever wrong?"

"It's been known to happen." Her thumb traced around the bottle's opening as slowly and deliberately as she toyed with her necklace.

Her pink lips were so kissable, so inviting, so damn close and getting closer with every inch he leaned toward her.

"Sean." She whispered his name as her eyelids began to drop and her mouth to open. She set her beer down on the coffee table with a hard clank—and foam rushed up the bottle's neck like a geyser and poured across the table. "Shit."

Sean grabbed the collar of his T–shirt behind his neck and yanked it over his head so he could use it as a towel to stop the flow of beer before it ran off the edge and onto the floor. He sopped up the suds, gathered the material into a ball, and hustled it over to the kitchen, where he dropped it with a wet thud into the stainless–steel sink.

Natalie sat as still as a statue on his couch, her eyes round with surprise and a flush turning her cheeks pink. "I'm sorry...I...uh..."

Only then did Sean realize he was now standing shirtless in front of his boss, the woman who he shouldn't give two rats' asses about but still wanted to impress.

You, Duvin, are doing a real fucking bang–up job of that.

Natalie refused to down the rest of her beer in one gulp, no matter how badly she wanted to relieve the hundred–year drought in her mouth.

Sean wasn't the first man she'd seen shirtless in all his Apollo–like glory and, God willing, he wouldn't be the last. Still, the sight of his six pack and hard pecs wouldn't be something she'd forget anytime soon and, for once, she couldn't think of a damn thing to say.

They just stared at each other, heat as potent as anything they brewed up at the Sweet Salvation Brewery nuking the air between them.

Look away, Natalie. Look away!

But she didn't. Even blinking became a crime against nature. She took in his broad, well–defined shoulders, the thick muscles curving his biceps, and the trail of dark hair that traveled from his bellybutton to behind the top button of his low–slung jeans. Her bra tightened, the unlined lace chaffing her hard nipples, and a honey–thick river of desire flowed through her veins until her heart pounded like a kettledrum in her ears.

"I'll be right back." Sean spun on his heel, his rubber–soled work boots squeaking against the polished wood floor, and took off up the metal staircase leading to the loft.

He was gone before the first embarrassed flush bloomed in her cheeks, but once it did, the sun paled in comparison to the heat making her face pulse. Her fingers flew across the pearl necklace in time with her rushed heartbeat, and her eyes darted around Sean's house.

The exposed bricks that should look worn and dirty instead seemed raw and unflinching. The unapologetic simplicity of the open–space design offered up a what–you–see–is–what–you–get vibe. Add to it the slate–gray, dusty–red, and wrought–iron color palette that didn't have even a dab of compromise. All of it together was a testosterone palace screaming out at Natalie that she didn't belong here.

Like she didn't know that already.

She needed to ignore the giddy feeling in her stomach that started whenever she was near Sean and finish what she came here to do. Then she could get the hell away from Sean, his dude's dude house, and his sinfully lick–o–licious abs.

Grabbing her red pen and her notebook, she blocked off a three–column chart, making the first column half the size of the other two. That felt better.

Nothing like a little organization to ease the uncertainty of life. Across the top she wrote Date, Problem and Those Present. The knot at the base of her neck loosened, and she rolled her head from shoulder to shoulder.

Next, she took her green pen and filled in the appropriate information to the best of her knowledge. She'd need to wait for Sean to double–check the complete listing of who was present when each event took place, but she could at least get the basics down. Humming to herself, she filling in the orderly columns with her neat handwriting. Her blood pressure settled back into its normal level—right in time for Sean's reappearance.

He hesitated at the base of the steps and her pulse did a quick jig. She tightened her grip on the green pen.

He'd put on a black Sweet Salvation Brewery shirt, covering up the miles of sinewy muscles—the memory of which would take an atom–splitting blast to dislodge from her brain.

"Sorry." He ran his hands through his thick hair, pushing the waves away from his face and exposing the small scar above his eye—the same one that reminded her of something she couldn't remember. The more she tried to bring the shimmery recollection into the light, the further it faded into the background.

"Sorry for what?" Being uber hot and utterly frustrating?

He shrugged. "I overreacted about the beer."

"Don't sweat it. The floors look amazing. If it was my house, I'd have probably taken off my shirt to save them too." Oh my God! What was she saying? *Change the subject, now, Natalie.* "Soooo..." She drew out the word into several syllables while she fumbled for something to say. The notebook on the coffee table snagged her attention. "I made a chart so we could see if there was any overlap on people at each accident site."

"Of course you did." Sean crossed the room in a few long–legged strides and sat down beside her on the couch.

Having him so near turned her brain to mush again and she reached up for the comfort of her pearl necklace.

He wrapped his fingers around her hand, stopping her before her fingers reached their destination. "What's the story with the necklace?"

"It's a boring story." She gulped over the lump that had formed in her throat. "You don't want to hear it."

"I do." He squeezed her hand, his thumb grazing the top in a circular motion that eased the tension eating away at her.

Part of her wanted to touch each pearl twelve times. The other part wanted nothing more than to steal a little of Sean's strength by continuing to hold his hand. Instead, she opted for sanity and slid her fingers from between his. She clasped her hands together in her lap, anchoring herself to reality. "So you know about my family, right?"

He nodded his head.

"Yeah, they aren't your typical family. Running moonshine, stealing cattle, drunk and disorderly, public protests, and, according to rumor, my grandmother burned down the local Department of Motor Vehicles." MeMaw had sworn six ways to Sunday that she hadn't done it. The fire marshal determined an electrical short had started the blaze, but the good people of Salvation rarely remembered that part. "Plus my Uncle Julian lobbied Ruby Sue for years to add pot to her pecan pie. He said it was the only thing that could make it better. Like I said, not typical."

"I'd call it..." Sean stared at the ceiling while he no doubt searched for the right euphemism for crazy. "Unique."

"That's one word for it." She chuckled. "But if you were the kind of kid who made her first organizational chart in Crayola in pre–school, you'd understand how off–putting that kind of chaotic life could be. I had my first anxiety attack in middle school. I hyperventilated during the science fair when my dad got into a fight with the principal about the school canceling the drama program. Olivia was big into that and it wasn't fair that they'd cut funding for no good reason."

That night was seared into her brain. The embarrassment. The panic. The weight of all those judgmental eyes staring right at her. The incident had exposed a crack in her foundation that would only get worse.

Sean reached out and covered her white–knuckled hands. So grateful for the understanding, she almost broke apart but pulled back just in time.

Taking a deep breath, she continued. "My anxiety got worse from then on, but I had my sisters with me all the time. We were like the Three Musketeers, standing together against a town that didn't much like our family and, by association, us." It hadn't been a fun time, but she'd survived. Foolishly, she'd thought the anxiety would disappear as soon as she left Salvation. "Then I went to college, far away from home and my sisters. Halfway through the first semester, I had an anxiety attack so bad I couldn't leave my dorm room for two weeks. Long story short, Miranda found a therapist who came to see me. Without Dr. Kenning, I'm not sure I would have ever left that room on my own power."

She slid a hand free of Sean's comfort and ran her fingers across the necklace. "Dr. Kenning gave me the necklace at the end of my intensive therapy, as a sort of graduation gift. So now you know, I'm just as kooky as the rest of the Sweets."

He squeezed her hand and leaned in close, resting his forehead against hers. "Normal is overrated."

"Oh, but wouldn't it be nice for a change?" She laughed, breaking the spell. An awkwardness seeped into her bones. Only a few people knew the story behind the necklace, and now Sean was one of them. That she'd opened up to him...well, it scared her. Maybe there really was more to him than she'd first thought.

She offered him a strained smile. "Enough about my mysterious necklace. We have a brewery to save."

He raised an eyebrow at her forced cheer but seemed to play along. Her heart hiccuped in her chest. Damn.

He pulled out a sheaf of papers from the stack he carried. "I hit pay dirt in my office."

She straightened in her seat. "What did you find?"

"The accident reports for the other incidents over the past two weeks." A sheepish smile took over his normally taciturn expression. "They were at the bottom of the third pile I looked through."

"Great." She took the papers, careful to keep her fingers from brushing his—again. For her own self–

preservation, she needed a safety bubble when it came to Sean O'Dell or she'd end up falling for him and that couldn't happen. "Why don't I check them out while you add who was around when each accident occurred into the chart."

He picked up the blue pen and the notepad from the coffee table.

"Not that pen." She grabbed his wrist and a warm tingling sensation danced across her skin, burning her in the best way. So much for her safety bubble. "Here." She held out the green pen. "Use this one." Her voice sounded off to her own ears.

"Why?"

"Because the blue one is for suspects only." Surely he could see that, the logic was apparent. "Color coding allows you to take in information at only a glance. It's very efficient."

He raised an eyebrow and gave her the same look people on the subway gave to the guy wearing an aluminum hat and talking to his Hello Kitty watch.

She was about to launch into a mini–lecture about the many studies that had been done on the subject when he dropped the blue pen and accepted the green one. She mentally did a happy dance. "Thanks."

He gave her a questioning look. "For what?"

"For not making me feel weird." About the reports, about her habits, about the beer, about pretty much everything that had most folks giving her the side eye.

"There's plenty weird about you, but all in a good way." He turned serious. "Point me in the direction of anyone who ever tells you different and I'll knock sense into them."

Unsure what to say when a flock of butterflies had taken flight in her stomach, she picked up the thick stack of accident reports, determined to get lost in the welcoming arms of data.

A half–hour later, she collapsed back against the cool leather of Sean's couch. He relaxed beside her, his shoulder touching hers, the contact sending delightful shivers across her skin. His touch might—okay, did—distract her, but not enough to pull her completely away from the task at hand. Few things did. It was one of the things that had helped her become one of the top efficiency consultants in the country. She was always about the task at hand.

"Please tell me you're seeing some overlap of employees in the chart because I have a big fat goose egg after going through the accident reports."

Sean shook his head. "Some folks keep showing up, but we have a small staff, so it's bound to happen."

"Who do you have?" The answer was there, they just weren't seeing it yet.

"Well, Billy was at the fermentation tank before it started leaking, but he just got ten stitches in the head from the nozzle valve switch."

Billy was relatively new and still familiarizing himself with the ins and outs of the brewery. To say the goofy kid had a bad case of hero worship when it came to Sean was an understatement. Billy spent most of his time following the brewmaster around like a puppy dog hoping to hear "good boy" from its owner.

"I don't buy it," she said. "Who else?"

"Hailey, but she's been with the brewery long before I ever got there, and your Uncle Julian always seemed to trust her more than anyone else."

Plus she understood the value of color coding. That was always a mark in favor in Natalie's world. "It has to be someone."

"What if it's someone who used to work at the brewery?" he asked.

"Like Carl?" Just mentioning the former brewmaster's name pissed her off. "He's still in the county lockup. His wife can't make bail."

Sean snorted. "More like his wife's family can't make bail."

"What do you mean?"

"She's a Peterson. Her parents own a big chunk of Salvation County."

"You don't think she asked for their help?" Natalie asked.

"Probably asked, doubtful she got it." He took off his cap and ran his long fingers through his thick hair.

"Why?"

"Rumor is her family objected to the marriage."

Juicy stuff, but not the right kind of information she was after, which was really starting to annoy her. Every problem had a solution, and with enough time, she'd find the one to who was sabotaging the brewery. The only question was, did she have the time? "Will Billy be back at work tomorrow?"

Sean shook his head. "Gave him the day off."

"Okay, let's plan on chatting with Hailey tomorrow. Maybe she saw something she didn't realize was important at the time." Natalie gathered her pens and her notebook and slid them into her bag. The crinkle of paper being crumpled reminded her of what else she'd brought with her. She took out the three pieces of paper. "I was going through the personnel files today and noticed your W–2 wasn't in the file. I brought you another one you can fill out real quick."

He drummed his fingers on the coffee table. "I'll do it later."

"Might as well get it over with." She handed him a black pen. "Anyway, bringing it in tomorrow will give me an excuse to—"

Before she could even get the words "talk to Hailey" out, Sean's lips came down on hers.

Desperation to get her to stop asking him to fill out the W–2 had pushed Sean into the kiss, but it was going to take a tow truck to pull him away. She tasted too good, felt too right, and moaned too sweetly for the realization that this was all wrong to pierce the lust fogging his better judgment.

She relaxed opened up beneath him, and tasting her was like getting a glimpse of heaven. But Sean wanted more than a view from the cheap seats. Without ever losing contact with her hungry mouth, he tangled his fingers into the knot of hair at the top of her head and found the metal clip holding it all in place. Gripping it between his forefinger and thumb, he slowly pulled it out of the light–brown mass. Her hair fell down in waves, overflowing his hands and falling past her shoulders to the small of her back. His hands followed the trail to the perfect rise of her ass that filled his hands.

All he wanted to do was get lost in Natalie. He'd carry her upstairs to his king–size bed, lay her down in the middle of his sheets, and lick every inch of her until she broke apart in his arms and cried out for mercy. Then he'd make her do it again.

He sucked the juicy fullness of her bottom lip into his mouth, lightly raking his teeth across the tender flesh. The woman he'd too often thought of as a thorn in his side shivered in his arms. The need to touch her everywhere steamrolled over any objections. He brought his hands around front to the tiny buttons on her sweater.

Deepening the kiss, he slid his tongue into her welcoming mouth just as his fingers closed on the button at the bottom of her cardigan and slipped it free. He followed the soft material north to the next fastened button, but she'd beat him to it.

"No," he whispered against her mouth.

Her hands stilled, but her chest heaved. "Why?"

Removing the button from her grasp, he slipped it through the hole. "I have spent way too much time thinking about what it would be like to unbutton each one of these."

Not satisfied to remain a passive partner, she snuck her hands under his T–shirt. "You think about that, huh?"

"Every damn day." The woman had taken up residence in his thoughts the first day she arrived at the brewery with her clipboard. He was beyond fighting the attraction.

Her touch against his abs was the best kind of torture, and the bulge pushing against his zipper grew. How many times had he stroked himself while fantasizing about this exact moment? How many times had his balls tightened in anticipation? How many times had he finished alone but remained hungry for more—for the real thing? For only Natalie?

Three buttons down, two more to go. Torn between the release of going faster and the anticipation of taking it slow, he bought time by trailing his lips down the creamy column of her neck.

"And does thinking about it make you hard?" Her thumb, and only her thumb, rubbed up and down the length of his zipper.

The contact destroyed and rebuilt him with every stroke. "Like concrete."

Her lips rested against his earlobe, close enough that moisture from her breath evaporated against his overheated skin. "Just because of a row of buttons?"

"No, because of what you keep hidden away from the world behind this conservative facade." The last button was all that remained.

"What makes you think it's an act?"

"Right now?" He slipped the last button free. The small amount of blood not concentrated in his dick pounded against his eardrums. "A whole lotta hope."

"I'd say it's time to test your hypothesis."

He parted her cardigan, revealing the world's most perfect tits, practically overflowing a deep–purple see–through lace bra. The top curve of her dusky–peach areolas peeked above the plunging cut of the bra, and her hard nipples pushed against the lacy prison. He slowly swept his thumb across a pointed tip. Her soft mewl of pleasure made him want to beat his chest caveman style and stake his claim.

Which was exactly why he had to stop. A man in hiding couldn't afford to grow attached, not when he might have to get lost fast.

Pulling back, he gulped in a breath of honeysuckle air. Instead of lessening the hunger, the flowery smell only drove home just how much he wanted her beneath him, on top of him, beside him—he didn't care, as long as he was buried inside her.

It took every ounce of self–control he had to rest his forehead against hers instead of following his instinct to throw her over his shoulder and carry her upstairs. Eyes closed and jaw clenched, he shut down the want ravaging him.

"Sean." Her breathy voice caressed his skin, taunting him with her closeness. "What just happened?"

He couldn't open his eyes. If he saw her this close, at this moment, he didn't think he'd be able to hold off. "I kissed you."

"Is that what the kids are calling it these days?" Firmer now, her tone sounded more like the no–nonsense efficiency expert turning his life upside down. Still, her fingers fisted his T–shirt like a woman barely hanging on herself, and she hadn't made a move to put space between them. "Why?"

Because he was Sean Duvin, not Sean O'Dell. Because he couldn't fill out a W–2 without Rupert Crowley and the other entrainment reporter jackals finding him. But that wasn't really why he'd done it. Deep down, he knew he'd kissed her because even as frustrating as she was, Natalie made him forget all of that. She made him believe Sean Duvin had never existed. That the person he was trying so hard to be was who he really was.

"It just happened," he said. A strand of her hair tickled his cheek, but there was no way he was easing back even a millimeter.

"Uh–huh. Look, despite what 'just happened', we can't do this." She still hadn't moved away, and her fingers tangled in his shirt were so close to his bare flesh underneath that a piece of paper couldn't fit between them.

"Why not?" He kept his hands still, afraid the smallest movement would send her flying away.

"I'm your boss. It's wrong."

"So why haven't you moved?" And for that matter, why hadn't he? The simple truth was, he didn't want to.

"Because wanting and needing aren't always the same thing."

"Ain't that a bitch?"

"Yeah, it is." She released her grip on his shirt and laid one palm against his fast–beating heart. "I have to go."

The announcement sliced somewhere deep inside him. "Do you?"

She chuckled, a bittersweet sound that twisted his gut, and pushed him away. It didn't take much. He was on his feet a second later, his hands shoved in his pockets to stop from reaching for her.

Natalie buttoned her cardigan in no time flat, picked up her bag, leaving the unfilled–out W–2 in the middle of his otherwise bare coffee table, and grabbed her coat from the back of the couch. "About what happened, it's probably best..."

"Don't worry." He took her coat from her and held it up so she could slide her arms into the sleeves. "I'm not a big talker."

Zipping up her coat, she turned to face him. "Yeah, I've noticed."

He opened his mouth to deliver a rejoinder, but she brushed her lips across his in the briefest of kisses, stealing the words from his mouth. Then she opened the door and walked out into the cold night.

The teasing scent of her honeysuckle perfume lingered in the air behind her, the innocence of it reminding him of just how many dark secrets he was hiding.

Chapter Eight

The next morning, Natalie edged forward in her office chair and read the same e–mail for the hundredth time in the past five minutes. How had the Salvation gossip mill been so very wrong?

Even Ruby Sue at The Kitchen Sink didn't know about this, and she was Salvation's equivalent of the NSA when it came to uncovering the town's secrets. Natalie's fingers flew up and down her strand of pearls like a nun with rosary beads and glanced down at the calendar from The Organizational Outlet on her desk.

The dates lined up.

It made perfect sense.

Yet she couldn't shake the feeling that something was off.

A light tap on her office door snapped her attention away from the screen and onto someone who made her heart palpitate for an entirely different reason.

Sean filled her doorway in his uniform of jeans—slightly worn in all the right places, a Sweet Salvation Brewery T–shirt tugged tight across his broad shoulders, and baseball cap pulled low on his forehead. The cap hid his eyes but not the full lips that should be illegal on a man. And especially her employee.

Her thighs tingled at the memory of *that* kiss last night and the feel of his hard length underneath her thumb. Without meaning to, her gaze dropped to his zipper and she licked her lips.

"Morning, Sean!" Hailey called out cheerfully as she passed Natalie's open office door. "Nat, did Sean give you..." She looked down at the papers crumpled in Sean's white–knuckled fist. Her head snapped up and she looked at Natalie. Her eyes rounded before she glanced back at Sean. "Uh...yeah...so...bye."

The office manager sped down the hallway, her heels clacking a hasty retreat on the linoleum floor.

An embarrassed awkwardness bloomed on Natalie's cheeks. That in itself was pretty damn weird. But every other reaction she had around the steamy–hot brewmaster was completely out of whack. Why not how she'd react to him after he'd gotten to second base?

He cleared his throat and held up a thin stack of papers. "I found the quality control reports for the past six months."

That brought her right back to the problem at hand. The reports were the least of their worries right now. There was trouble at the Sweet Salvation Brewery. It started with C, and that stood for Carl. "He's not in jail."

"Who?"

"Carl." Just saying the former brewmaster's name out loud brought her full circle back to annoyed confusion. "He's not in jail."

Something a few degrees short of flame–thrower–level anger darkened Sean's face, and he stepped inside her small office, shutting the door behind him. "Rewind."

She pointed at her computer. "Come see for yourself."

He strolled to her side and bent over her left shoulder to read the e–mail displayed on her screen. Natalie realized her mistake as soon as he stood next to her, close enough that she could get high off his so–bad–for–you–they're–too–good–to–pass–up pheromones. The words on the screen turned blurry as she fought to concentrate on basic tasks—like not drooling on her keyboard.

"So our man Carl isn't in the pokey." Sean scooted closer, moving her mouse to scroll down on her screen.

The move put them nearly cheek–to–cheek and set off a series of fizzy pops in her stomach. "His wife posted bail seven days ago."

"Now he's on the lam." His words sent a loose tendril of hair airborne and it tickled the sensitive skin beneath her earlobe.

Her first instinct was to tuck it back into the simple fishtail braid curling over one shoulder, but she couldn't do it. Not with him this close. The chance of reaching out to finish what they'd started last night had gone from possible to probable the second he'd knocked on her door, and if she made a move it would skyrocket to highly likely.

Inhaling a shaky breath, Natalie ignored the displaced hair. "He missed his first court appearance this morning."

Sean ground his teeth together as his eyes narrowed. "And the idiots at the sheriff's office are just now getting around to notifying us that he made bail in the first place?"

"Pretty much." She shrugged.

Things obviously hadn't changed that much in Salvation, despite Miranda being engaged to the town's unofficial prince charming. Most of the people here still considered the Sweet family Salvation's equivalent of the weird neighbor who vacuumed naked with the shades open. Short of using the little flashy thing in the *Men in Black* movies to wipe everyone's memories of all the crazy things her family had done—including the fact her great-grandmother had celebrated her ninetieth birthday by getting busted for running moonshine—there wasn't a damn thing she could do to change folks' minds about her family.

Sean muttered some choice words under his breath and jerked upright. "I'm going down there."

"Wait." Without thinking, she slapped her hand on his, trapping him by her side.

The physical contact sucked the oxygen out of the room. Damn, she was really regretting not finishing what they started last night. All she should have been thinking about was stopping that asshole Carl from fucking with her brewery, but naughty thoughts about how to get into Sean's pants—and what she'd do once she got there—kept worming their way in.

Not wanting to, but needing to as much as she needed to keep air in her lungs, she slid her hand away from his. "Storming the sheriff's office won't make a bit of difference." Her voice barely registered a quake. Thank God for small favors. "The deputies have had enough dealings with my family over the years to justifiably hold a grudge. Going in guns blazing won't be the thing to change their minds."

Sean grabbed her chair by the armrests and spun her around and leaned in close enough that she could pick out the individual hairs on his beard. Concern and something else simmered behind his warm brown eyes. "But he's got to be the one messing things up at the brewery."

"Exactly." She placed one fingertip to his chest and gave him the slightest of pushes. He stepped back, giving her room to breathe. The protective–alpha–dog thing had taken her simmering lust and kicked it up a few thousand degrees. Fighting to maintain an outward appearance of complete control, she inhaled a cleansing breath and focused on the plan instead of the man. "We just have to catch Carl in the act."

"Why?"

"Because they're not going to believe a Sweet otherwise."

"How?" He shot her a skeptical look.

Damn, the man needed to learn to trust her. She sat up straighter in her chair, confidence in her solution as strong and sure as Paul Bunyan on steroids. "An old–fashioned stakeout."

"You watch too many movies." He yanked off his ball cap and twisted it in his hands like a wet dishrag.

"I don't watch movies."

He blinked at her in surprise. "Ever?"

"Not since I was a teenager. It's not really my thing." She gave him a hard look. "Stop trying to change the subject."

"This is crazy."

"No." Natalie shook her head, sending the loose hair bouncing. "It makes perfect sense."

"How's that?" He tucked the tendril behind her ear, his fingers lingering on the sensitive spot behind her lobe.

Her breath caught and for a split second she forgot what in the hell they'd been talking about as a shiver worked its way up from her core. The man was beyond dangerous.

"Because he's going to make another move," she said. "Think about it from his perspective. Uncle Julian promised Carl he'd get the brewery. Instead, Uncle Julian left it to me and my sisters. Then Miranda fires him. And when he decides to pay her back by running her off the road, he ends up behind bars. In the week he's been out, we've already had three incidents—one of which sent two people to the hospital. He's motivated, he's knowledgeable about the brewery, and he's accelerating."

Sean looked heavenward and sighed. "When?"

Finally. "I'm starting tonight."

"I'll be here." He loomed over her, his feet shoulder-width apart and his arms crossed over his mouthwateringly awesome chest. The curve of the biceps she'd felt last night peeked out from underneath his short sleeves. He may have given in to her argument, but judging by the take-no-shit look on his face, he wasn't done fighting.

A whole night.

Alone.

With Sean.

Her stomach dropped below sea level, which made sense, because her insides had all gone adrift at the mere idea of spending the night with Sean.

"You don't have to," she sputtered. "I'll watch everything on the security cameras, safe in my office."

Her hand barely trembled as she slid the cabinet door to the side, revealing a small TV. Images from the four cameras flickered on the screen in quick rotation.

"Those didn't pick up anything before," he scoffed.

Like she'd ever leave underperforming equipment in place. "I've made some adjustments."

"What do you mean?"

"See for yourself." She grabbed the remote out of her center desk drawer and punched a few buttons. The camera zoomed and refocused. The grainy image disappeared, replaced by a screen divided into four boxes with clear footage of a different part of the brewery in each one.

"Damn."

With the technology upgrade, she'd be able to spot an intruder and alert the authorities without ever leaving the safety of her locked office. "Yep. We have night–vision, motion–sensitive cameras now. So you see, you don't—"

He took the remote from her hand, his fingers brushing hers and setting off a mini–tsunami of desire. "Where'd they come from?"

"You don't want to know what all my Uncle Julian had in his garage." The two–car garage had been filled to the rafters with survival supplies, chain–link fencing, surveillance equipment and more. "It's like he was prepping for a zombie apocalypse."

He gave the remote a thorough looking over before handing it back to her. "Well then, I'll see you tonight." He pivoted and headed toward her closed office door.

"Sean, you don't—"

"Forget it, Natalie." He shoved his hat on his head. "I'll see you tonight."

Hungry and bordering on hangry, Sean walked into The Kitchen Sink ready for a pot roast sandwich served with an oversized helping of potato salad and a gallon of sweet tea. If he was lucky—a really big if—there'd still be a slice of pecan pie in the glass display case when he finished.

"Don't think you're getting by me." The voice, made low and wheezy by decades of smoking, stopped him before the diner's front door had even swung closed.

Ruby Sue sat in her usual spot on a high stool behind the cash register. She looked like the stereotypical little old lady, with her tight white curls and her thick glasses hanging from a chain around her neck. Sean knew better. The woman was a restaurant owner, gossip mastermind, and PhD-level pot stirrer. She'd seen through him the first night he'd rolled into town looking for a warm meal and a menial job. He'd washed dishes in the back for three months before she'd manipulated Julian into hiring him at the brewery.

Fact was, Sean owed Ruby Sue. And she knew it.

"Now why would I want to do that, Ruby Sue?"

"Come on, there's a corner booth open." She made a half-snort, half-honk sound, grabbed her purse, and sidled down off her stool. "We wouldn't want any of these rumor mongers to listen in."

It took everything he had, but Sean managed not to laugh out loud at her sass. She was like the housekeeper in the original *Parent Trap* movie who always swore she "never said nothing about nobody" and then managed to tell everything about everybody.

Still, he followed her spry shuffle across the crowded restaurant, past the packed lunch counter, and to an empty booth in the far corner.

She took the seat with the back to the wall. All the better to keep an eye on her customers and the front door. "Sit."

"Yes, ma'am." He slid into the seat across from her already set up with silverware wrapped in a white paper napkin.

Ruby Sue leaned forward on her elbows, gave a shifty–eyed look toward the lunch crowd, and dropped her voice. "Is it that fool Carl Brennan? His mama tried to steal my pecan pie recipe when she worked here. They say the apple doesn't fall far from the tree."

"That's what they say about the Sweets."

"Whoever's saying that obviously doesn't know shit from Shinola." Her eyes crinkled at the corner. "But you sure are awfully protective of that family...or at least one Sweet in particular from what I hear."

He shifted in his seat and fidgeted with the wrapped silverware. "I don't know what you're talking about."

"I always liked that Natalie Sweet. Girl's got fortitude."

He kept his attention focused on the silverware now held in a tight grip. He couldn't look at Ruby Sue. She took in too much at a glance.

"Here's Ellen. Do you want the regular?" She glanced up at the redheaded waitress making a beeline toward them while holding a giant glass of sweet tea in each hand.

He nodded.

Ellen placed the condensation–covered plastic glasses on the table.

"Boy, it wouldn't kill you to step out of your comfort zone every once in a while," Ruby Sue said.

He didn't bother trying to smother his laugh this time. That advice coming from Ruby Sue was like hearing Dixieland jazz from a punk rock band. "Have you been watching the daytime talk shows again?"

"Hush your mouth." She ripped open three packets of sugar and poured them into her already diabetic–coma–inducing glass of the sweet stuff. "He'll have the pot roast on a hoagie with extra potato salad. I'm good."

"You should eat," he urged. "It's lunchtime."

The look she gave him would have made his old cold–blooded Hollywood agent take a few steps back. "I'll take that under advisement."

The waitress gave him a what–can–you–do shrug and ambled off to the kitchen to place his order.

Ruby Sue took three large drinks of spiked sweet tea, five years coming off her face with each swallow, before beginning her interrogation. "Okay, spill it."

He filled her in on the troubles at the brewery and the fact that all signs pointed to the permanently pissed–off former brewmaster.

Ruby Sue shook her head. “Make a decision in haste and repent on your own time.”

“Come again?” he asked.

“Joni Peterson was a wild child. Her mama and daddy warned her. Hell, half the town warned her about Carl Brennan, but she was too headstrong to listen. She tied her wagon so tight to Carl that she cut off contact with her family. Her daddy died a year ago. Cancer finally got her mother a few weeks ago.” She poured another pack of sugar into her sweet tea, stirring it with her straw until the white granules dissolved. “Seems bad news and old gossip always circles back around.”

“What do you mean?” Cold air blasted up his spine even though they weren’t anywhere near the front door.

“Fella came in the other day flashing an old photo of a young man.” Ruby Sue watched him from over the rim of her glass. “Thought at first he was some sort of private investigator looking for a deadbeat, then he gave me his card.”

She fished a business card out of her purse and slid it across the table. *Hollywood and Vine Reports* was written in purple calligraphy across the top. He didn’t have to look closely at the photo in the bottom left corner to see the man’s botox–injected forehead, blinding–white smile, and empty eyes.

Sean’s time in Salvation was up.

Rupert Crowley had found him and was closing in for the kill.

Everything inside him froze in place and he automatically clicked over into a sort of detached survival mode. He knew it well. It’s exactly how he’d survived the first years of his life. He’d won an Oscar at twenty–one for a very good reason. He’d been acting his whole life. It had been the best way to avoid his father's fists.

"I gotta go." He stood and was reaching for his wallet before the sentence was even out of his mouth.

"This Rupert fella said he was tracking down an actor who'd fallen off the face of the earth." Ruby Sue didn't make a move to stop him, but her flinty blue eyes took in his every move. "Said he was working on a where–are–they–now piece and would pay good money to anyone who could point him in the right direction."

"Huh," he grunted. Whatever the sleazeball gossip reporter was working on, Sean sure as hell wasn't interested.

"Asked me if I knew of a Sean Duvin. Told him I'd never met anyone by that name."

She may not know exactly why he was hiding or who from, but she wouldn't give him up. Of that he was one–hundred–percent confident.

"And you won't." Sean tossed a ten and a five on the table. That should cover the sandwich he wasn't going to eat and Ellen's tip. "Sean Duvin doesn't exist anymore."

Sean's SUV idled at the stop sign on the edge of Salvation. His left turn signal ticked in a steady rhythm like a time bomb.

The savvy move would be to turn left, go home, pack up, and disappear in another small town. Crowley wouldn't have left the bright lights of the big city and traveled across the country to small–town Virginia unless he was damn sure he'd find Sean here—and he wouldn't leave until he'd confirmed he'd found him.

Tick.

Tick.

Tick.

There was plenty of gossip in Tinseltown, but the reporter had dogged Sean's footsteps for years, writing too many magazine articles and televised reports to count and even publishing a book about the "talented young actor who'd vanished from the face of the Earth." Crowley had built up Sean to be this generation's James Dean just without the dead body inside a twisted car's wreckage.

Tick.

Tick.

Tick.

A car horn blared behind him. Sean rolled down the driver's side window and waved the minivan around. The soccer mom gave him a one–fingered salute and peeled off toward the right. Following the van with his gaze, he leaned forward until he could see the Sweet Salvation Brewery turnoff. Natalie waited two miles down that asphalt road.

Long answers to short questions. Soft sweaters with tiny little buttons. The clipboard always at the ready. Hungry lips and soft moans. Tightly wound hair. The teasing scent of honeysuckle that followed in her wake. Five–billion–point plans. Endless possibilities.

Tick.

Tick.

Tick.

He glanced the other direction at the open highway. Freedom and anonymity lived along that road. All he had to do was turn left and Sean Duvin would stay buried. Maybe forever if he did a good enough job of running. He was good at disappearing. Always had been. He'd been eight years old the first time he'd lost himself in a role, escaping his frustrated actor slash domineering stage father and the backhands that came out of nowhere for no reason. After that, he'd never looked back.

He couldn't afford to now.

But the idea of leaving Natalie while someone was doing their damnedest to sabotage the brewery left a foul taste in his mouth, sour without any hint of sweet. He couldn't fucking do it.

Truth was, he was tired of play acting at being himself.

Easing his foot off the break, the SUV rolled into the intersection before making a right turn and heading toward the brewery and Natalie.

Chapter Nine

With four hours to go until most of the brewery staff left, Natalie was officially going stir–crazy waiting for something—anything—to go wrong. If she stayed another minute in her office, she was going to start accessorizing with a straightjacket instead of pearls.

Armed with her clipboard, her red pen, and the anxiety jitters reminiscent of downing ten shots of espresso, she marched out of her office on a mission. She'd find Sean, work out a schedule for the stakeout tonight, and plot a course of action for when they found the son of a bitch messing with her brewery.

Turning the corner, she crossed into Sean's office. "Hey, about tonight." She looked up from her clipboard and almost dropped it.

The office was empty.

And clean.

"Holy shit," she muttered to herself as she walked in slow motion around the space.

The paper towers were gone, as were the coffee mugs that had littered Sean's desk. The overturned pen holder had been righted and filled. The stack of brochures sat in the inbox with the brewers invitational on top. He'd said last night that he'd found the paperwork in the third pile he searched, but she hadn't thought...

She shuffled over to the filing cabinets. Only the smallest line of sticky residue remained of the tape holding the drawers shut yesterday. Wondering if it was a dream, she yanked open the top drawer. Perfectly organized files filled it. They weren't color–coded, but it was a start.

"Not one word." Sean stood in the doorway, one shoulder propped up against the doorframe and his mouth sealed in a straight line.

Natalie blinked in surprised and opened her mouth.

He held up his hand. "I mean it."

He had to be kidding. It was a total office makeover. He deserved high praise. "But it's so—"

"I'll take all the paper out and scatter it." It wasn't an idle threat. The stubborn man would do it.

She preached the gospel of organization and efficiency with the zeal of a born–again devotee. She couldn't let that happen. So instead of a well–deserved "I told you so", she pursed her lips and mimicked locking them closed with a pretend key that she tossed over her shoulder.

Shaking his head, he pushed off the doorframe and strutted across the room, stopping a foot from the filing cabinets. Too far away to touch, but too close to ignore the tension winding up her insides like a rubber band airplane. Unable to have what she wanted, Natalie clutched her clipboard close enough that the metal clip scratched her collarbone, a discomfort that registered dimly in the back of her mind.

Sean moved closer, slid the clipboard free from her grasp, and turned it over to read. "What's on the agenda today?"

Yielding ground to give herself breathing room, the back of her thighs hit Sean's desk. *Pull it together, girl.* "A schedule for tonight, a contingency plan for if he shows up, and another one for if he doesn't."

He flipped through the pages. "You're kidding, right?"

Why would she be? She'd never been a girl to leave things to chance and she wasn't starting now. "No."

Sean tossed the clipboard over her head. It landed on the desk with a clatter and skidded to the edge, teetering for a second before staying put on the flat surface. "You need to focus on something else."

"I can't." She twisted around to grab her clipboard, feeling as lost without it as an alien in rush–hour traffic.

Before she could grasp it, he took her by the hand and pulled her toward the door. "Come on."

Heated electricity tingled up her arm, dancing across her skin, danger and a comfort jolted her system. "Where?"

"My office."

"We're in your office." She took one last glance around before crossing into the hallway.

He turned, his face only inches from hers, an icy determination in his eyes. "No. The real one."

Calling the Sweet Salvation Brewery's reference library a "room" was being kind. Roughly the same size as Natalie's walk–in closet, the room had books about everything from the history of hops to the modern brewery operations and everything in between. A worn stool sat in the corner next to a small table crowded with spiral notebooks and handwritten diagrams listing various beer ingredients' properties.

When she'd first gotten to the brewery, she'd poured over the books to better understand how breweries worked. Then she'd moved on to the internet and interviewing everyone from other brewery owners to the staff at the National Craft Brewers Association.

Sean followed her inside and shut the door behind them. He stayed by the door, but in the tiny room the distance was more an illusion than a reality. In actuality, he filled the space from wall to wall until even the idea of him pushed against her, as tangible as the books on the shelves.

Awareness of him jolted through her body, as if she had a sixth sense for hotness. It made her jittery and unsure. Two of her least favorite feelings. She backed up until her ass hit the table's edge. Shit, she was doing that a lot around him.

Floundering for words—something else that happened whenever he was near—she blurted out the first thing that came to mind that didn't involve her licking his abs. "So this is one of the places besides the cooler where you hole up whenever I'm looking for you."

God, it seemed so obvious now. No one would be calling her Sherlock anytime soon.

He shrugged. "Pretty much."

He slouched against one of the bookshelves, his brown–eyed gaze locked on her. Though his body language was relaxed, an underlying sexual tension came off him in waves.

And damn her, she wanted to drown in him. Another place, another man, Natalie would be planning which item of clothing to discard first. But he was an employee and she couldn't cross that line with him again.

Needing to touch something, she raised her hand to her necklace and rubbed one pale pearl between her fingers. "Why are we here?"

"You need to be distracted before your head explodes." The too–knowing smile curling one side of his delicious mouth showed that he knew exactly how much he'd thrown her off balance. "I'm working on the stout recipe that will win the Southeast Brewers Invitational. I'm making small batches to test out each recipe, and this is where I come up with combinations to try out."

Falling into research mode, she relaxed. "How does that work?"

Sean pushed away from the bookshelf and joined her by the table. Standing only inches in front of her, he let his dark gaze dropped to her mouth.

So much for getting comfortable. Her heart jackhammered against her rib cage. There were a dozen reasons why she should leave now, but standing so close to him, none of them seemed to matter.

Leaning forward, his arm snaked around her, close enough that his bare forearm brushed against her waist as he reached for something on the table.

Her breath caught. It would have taken an earthquake to move her even the barest inch as she inhaled his clean–soap scent mixed with the brewery's distinctive hoppy aroma. Somewhere between inhalation and exhalation, she gave up the ghost. While she hadn't moved a millimeter, inside she felt like one of those animated gifs declaring "My body is ready."

"First..." His whisper tickled her ear. "You have to figure out what kind you're making." Sean pulled a red spiral notebook from behind her and took half a step back.

He stood far enough that she could make an escape if she wanted but close enough that she didn't want to. He flipped open the notebook but kept staring at her, not even trying to temper the lust swirling in his brown eyes.

The man was a first–class tease.

Remembering the night before at his house and the experimental beer, followed by him shirtless and the kiss that had burned its way into her forever memory, a slow shiver worked its way up her spine. "You're making a stout."

"Right." He reached up and drew her fingers away from her pearl necklace, sending an atom–bomb–level frisson of need through her body. "What makes a stout a stout?"

Fighting her way through the zero–visibility fog in her brain, she sputtered out the first answer she could come up with. "It's thick and has a foamy top?"

"Not foam, a head." He laughed and stroked his thumb down the center of her palm before releasing it. He squeezed his eyes closed, clenched his jaw shut and gulped. After a deep breath, he reopened his eyes and sidestepped her so they stood shoulder to shoulder.

At least she wasn't the only one affected. Triumph and relief battled inside her as she pivoted to face the table.

He laid the notebook on the table and flipped to a page filled with his cramped, printed writing. "Usually, a stout is an opaque black or brown with dark–red highlights. A typical dry stout has a roasted, grainy sharpness, a hint of unsweetened chocolate, and a bitter bite from the hops. The one I'm working on has a touch of an acidic sourness too."

Natalie made the bitter–beer face, as if she'd just sucked a lemon.

That made him laugh out loud. The sound released some of the sexual tension stringing both of them tight. "Don't make that face. It's a good kind of tart sour, not nasty sour like milk gone bad."

The warm sound of his voice was doing more to ease the worry curdling her lunch about tonight's stakeout than three trips up and down her pearl necklace. "Why a stout?"

"Ales and IPAs are everywhere, but there aren't that many small–craft beers that make a stellar stout that stands out. So it's good business sense for the Sweet Salvation Brewery." He said it as if reciting a line he'd had to memorize.

The man needed to learn he didn't have to guard every piece of information as if it were the combination to Fort Knox. "But that's not all of it."

"No." He shook his head and spoke slowly, as if building up to something. "I like the strength of it. The stouts were created to capitalize on the porters that came first. The difference was the stouts were fuller, creamier, with more body and alcohol punch—though not so much anymore."

"And yours, will it have a higher alcohol content?"

"Not mine. Ours. Sweet Salvation Brewery's." The brewery's name came out in a rush. "And why not? It's a good differentiator—like an imperial ale's ten percent or more versus an IPA's five to seven percent."

"And the dry stout, is that what you're making?

"No."

She stared at his profile, but he'd lost himself in the notebook. "Are you gonna make me go find the great big book of beers back in my office so I can go through them all to make another guess on what kind of stout?"

He looked up, crossing his arms in front of his strong chest, his feet shoulder–width apart as if he were expecting a blow. "I'm making a hybrid of a dry stout and a Russian imperial stout."

For most people, that wouldn't be a revelation. But Sean wasn't most people. For some reason she couldn't quite grasp, he'd cracked open the door and was letting her in.

Natalie sank down onto the stool. "Go on."

He let out a deep breath and took off his baseball hat before running his fingers through his thick hair. "The Russian is rich and complex, with fruity esters and roasted grains, hops, and a coffee– or chocolate–flavored malt."

"Remember I'm still new. Fruity esters?"

He grabbed one of the books off the shelf and put it on the table between them. Opening it, he turned to the glossary. "Fruity esters. They're the compounds that give many fruits their characteristic flavors. We get them in beer by choosing the correct yeast for the recipe. In a Russian imperial stout, the fruity esters take on a dark–fruit character. Think raisins, plums, or prunes."

"So you want something that's sweet and sour."

He nodded, his gaze again dropping to her mouth. "Exactly."

The way he looked at her when she was fully dressed made her knees buckle. If he gave her that look while they were both naked, she might just climax on the spot. This man was far too dangerous. "What about cherry?"

"That might work." He stroked his beard, then grabbed a pencil and scrawled the word in the notebook. "I need to try that."

Hesitating only for a moment, Natalie decided to take advantage of Sean's unusually talkative mood. "So I love that we're finally talking brewery business, but why are you telling me this now?"

His pencil stilled. "I wanted to get you out of your controlled comfort zone and show you the brewery from another perspective." He laid it down on the table. "Plus, the more I talk, the less likely I am to do something stupid."

"Talking a lot." Natalie nudged him with her elbow. "That must feel strange."

He smiled. "It does."

Maybe she moved. Maybe Sean pulled her up from the stool. She couldn't be sure, but suddenly they were hip to hip and shoulder to shoulder. A small touch—minor really—but her breath caught as her entire body went on hyper alert. The clean–soap smell of him. The way his breath hitched then sped up. The underlying strength that called out to her, even when she tried to block it.

Sean pivoted to face her, the lust rampaging through her reflected in his own brown eyes, and the world stopped moving.

A heated flush rose up in tandem with the loud *thump–thump* of her heart vibrating through her body and she turned her face away so he wouldn't see. Every part of her tingled with anticipation of what would happen next. Not could. Would. She may be mentally denying what was going on between them, but her body sure as hell wasn't.

Still, the battle warred inside her head. She gripped the table and kept her gaze forward, knowing if she even snuck a sideways glance she'd fall—hard and completely. "What kind of stupid things are you trying to avoid?"

Ever so lightly, he grasped her chin and turned her to face him. "This."

His lips captured hers.

Soft and hard. Exhilarating and relaxing. Demanding and requesting. The kiss at his house had been an appetizer. This was the main course. She melted under this touch, her mouth opening for him. Not surrendering but returning his passion, matching his tongue stroke for stroke. He sucked her bottom lip into his mouth, pulling it taut then slowly loosening his hold.

Turning his attention to her neck, the dueling sensations of his soft lips and the scratch of his beard drove her nearly out of her mind. "And kissing me is stupid?"

He chuckled against her skin, the sensation tickling that magic spot where her neck met her shoulder. "Only if you're worried about my sanity, because I can't stop thinking about you as it is."

Pushing her fingers through his thick hair, she arched her head back to give him better access to her throat. "I know the feeling." Thoughts of him had haunted her since she'd returned to Salvation.

"Do you?" He teasingly nipped her collarbone before kissing it.

She shivered under his touch, desire dampening her panties and making her clench her thighs together in an attempt to find some relief. His devilish hands relaxed their grip on her hips and slid around to cup her ass, pulling her close. Thick, hard evidence of his desire pressed against her belly. God, she wanted this man, and not just to silent the stressful thoughts always swirling in her head. She wanted *him*, not just the divine moment of oblivion that blocked out everything else.

The realization scared her and brought some unwanted reality into the room. "We shouldn't be doing this."

"Why?" He made quick work of the buttons on her petal–pink cashmere sweater and parted her cardigan. Sean gave a soft growl as he stared at her silver satin pushup bra that presented her boobs like an all–you–can–lick buffet. "Because I'm your employee?"

He licked his lips and slid his thumb across the satin covering her hard nipple.

"Yes," she said, sighing. An answer to his question or a response to even the lightest of touches? Both.

"Easy fix." He snapped the front closure of her bra and her tits tumbled out. "I quit."

Bending forward, he lifted one heavy globe and took the hard nub into his hot mouth. Fire sizzled through her veins and it felt so good she couldn't wait to burn.

"You can't quit." She reached down for the top button of his jeans and flicked it open. "We need you. *I* need you."

He released her nipple and she groaned in frustration. Then he found the hem of her skirt and inched it higher and the soft groan that floated out of her mouth was for a whole other reason.

"Hire me back in about an hour or, better yet, a few days."

The cool air caressed her upper thighs as he raised her skirt, but it wasn't enough to relieve the molten heat engulfing her. "I like how you think."

He trailed a hand up the inside of her leg, sending a wave of need crashing through her. "I promise, you'll like other things even more."

"You wouldn't lie to a girl, would you?" She lowered his zipper and reached inside, wrapping her fingers around his hard girth.

"Never about this." He stopped a few inches shy of the juncture of her thighs and looked down at her, exposed before him. "Oh God. Do you wear these every day?" He traced the top of her thigh–high tights, his calloused thumb occasionally straying off the material to caress her bare thigh.

"You don't want to know the answer to that," she teased as she stroked up and down his length. "Maybe we should just get this attraction out of our system."

"You think then we can get back to normal after that?" He continued his upward exploration, pushing the center of her panties aside and sliding in first one and then a second finger.

The vibrations started in her thighs, expanding and growing with each in–and–out stroke. She squeezed her eyes shut to better concentrate on the feeling between her legs as he rolled his thumb over her clit, circling it in agonizingly pleasurable rotations.

"Yes. No." She groaned. "I can't think right now when you're touching me."

He laughed and increased the pressure, curling his fingers to rub against her G–spot. Rubbing. Twisting. Turning. "That means I'm doing it right."

Colors—oranges, pinks, whites—appeared in the darkness behind her closed lids, and the vibrations grew until she became a live wire personified.

"God, yes." She dropped her head onto his shoulder, the pleasure so great she couldn't do anything but let go and enjoy the ride as her climax broke.

Watching Natalie fall apart around his fingers, her wetness making her soft folds slick, was the sexiest thing Sean had ever seen. Her eyes remained closed, and the tension normally lining the corners of her mouth had drained from her face. Slowly he eased his fingers from her, hating the loss of contact.

Her eyes fluttered open, a satisfied smile turning her luscious lips upward. "You're a whole lot of trouble."

Pride filled him. He'd put that soft look in her eye, the purr in her voice, and given her loose limbed ease. Now he understood why the first caveman had risked life and limb to take down a saber–toothed tiger. Hunger for food had nothing to do with it.

"You haven't seen anything yet."

She shivered against him. "Is that a threat or a promise?"

His dick twitched. "Both."

Natalie shook out her hair and it fell in waves around her shoulders. "Normally—" she took a step back "—I'd love to chat, but I need you inside me."

He almost came from her words alone. Direct and to the point, his efficiency queen got straight to it. His dick ached from the torment of not touching her. "There's nothing I'd like more."

The rest of the words died in his mouth as she unzipped her skirt and dropped it to the floor. She stepped out of it and stood, hands on her curvy hips, now wearing only her glasses, silver bra, panties, and those thigh–highs that were going to give him a heart attack.

She shot him a saucy grin and strutted away from him and across the room to the door. Watching her round ass jiggle with each step had him hard enough to poke a hole in steel.

The click of the lock boomed across the room.

Turning, she leaned her back against the door, her long legs shoulder–width apart. "You were saying?"

"God, you're beautiful." He meant it. He'd seen a lot of naked women in his life. There were some perks to being a Hollywood heartthrob, but none lit up a room like Natalie.

Confident and more than a little cheeky, she winked. "That's what I thought."

This time she treated him to the vision of her swaying hips and amazing tits as she sashayed back to him and dropped to her knees, taking his jeans and boxers down with her.

The first touch of her tongue eliminated any possibility of more talk. The softness of her lips around his dick had him forgetting his own name. By the time she made the first downward stroke with her mouth, taking him all in, the rest of the world ceased to exist.

He tangled his hands in her hair, the silken strands spilling over his fingers and pouring over his thighs. He'd fantasied about this moment so many times as he'd stroked himself to completion, but none of his imaginings could even be a celluloid replica of the real thing.

Her pink tongue swirled around his dick on an upward stroke and he almost nutted right then. "Babe, you gotta stop."

Natalie's mouth turned into a perfect pout before she puckered her lips and blew a cool breath against his rock–hard length. The sensation almost sent him over the edge.

He yanked her up, but she snuck her hands under his shirt and danced her fingers across his chest.

"Tell me you have a condom," she said.

Yanking up his jeans enough to reach into his back pocket, he withdrew his wallet and removed a foil package. He rolled the condom on in record time.

"Sit down." She nudged his shoulders until he sank to the seat and straddled him, lining him up with her soft folds. "You ready?"

The sight of her alone had his balls tightening. "I may not last."

"That makes two of us." She sank down, enveloping his dick in her warmth.

He groaned, the sweetness of reality almost more than he could stand.

Her back flexed under his fingertips as she rode him, swirling her hips in time with the rocking motion. Up, down, back and forth, she took him higher and higher. They moved together, matching each other stroke for stroke as their hushed moans filled the room. He clapped his hands on her hips, bringing her down with more force. She arched her back, changing the angle and allowing him to drive deeper, to fill her completely.

A soft mewling sound escaped her lips and her nails dug into his shoulders before she snapped forward as her second climax rocketed through her.

Looking up at Natalie, her hair falling around her shoulders in light–brown waves as she bit down on her bottom lip in ecstasy, the extent of her beauty—inside and out—made him breathless. Something shifted in him, and he realized two things. One, he wasn't leaving Salvation. Two, this thing between them was far from over after this.

His balls tightened. "Natalie," he groaned in a harsh whisper full of tormented bliss.

His vision went black and he surged inside her one last time before his orgasm shook him as hard as a hurricane.

"Oh. My. God." Her chest heaved against him and she rested her head on his shoulder. "I am totally jellified."

"My apologies." He twisted a strand of her long, loose hair around his finger and feathered the end across her still–hard nipple. It puckered tighter, and it was all he could do not to take her nipple into his mouth and go for round two, but the sounds of the brewery had begun to intrude into their cocoon.

Everyone knew not to bother him when he was in the reference room, but that didn't mean it never happened. The last thing he wanted was for someone to walk in and see Natalie. He wouldn't put her in that situation.

She stood up and grabbed her clothes from the floor.

In less time than it took for him to recover the bones in his body—minus the one between his legs—and pull up his jeans, she was back in buttoned–up mode, albeit with her hair in a crooked, messy knot on top of her head.

"Damn, you're fast."

She giggled and tucked a few stray hairs behind her ears. "I think you just experienced that for yourself."

"Nah." He lowered his lips to hers and put everything he didn't know how to say into the brief kiss. "I saw a helluva lot more than that."

"Thank God I remembered to lock the door or a lot more people could have seen more of me than needed." She crossed the room and unlocked the door.

She'd barely finished the action when the door she was leaning against flew open, sending her sailing across the small room and against Sean's chest. He clamped his arms around her, steadying her before she could fall.

The door smacked against the bookshelf and Hailey burst into the office. Her eyes went wide and her gaze ping–ponged from Sean to Natalie and back again. "Carl Brennan is in the parking lot. He's drunk as a skunk and carrying a shotgun."

Chapter Ten

Natalie tore out of the reference room at a full gallop, sprinting across the brewery floor and out into the tasting room. Almost every person who worked at the brewery stood with their noses pressed to the floor–to–ceiling front windows. She had to go up on her tiptoes to see over the crowd and spot Carl in the parking lot.

He ambled aimlessly around, bent–legged like he was on a whaler in rough waters. The whole thing might have been somewhat amusing if he wasn't dragging a long–barreled shotgun in his weaving wake.

"Shit," Sean mumbled under his breath.

"My thoughts exactly." Heart thumping in her ears, she skidded to a stop at the bar, grabbed the phone, and dialed 911.

Sean rushed to the front door. "Everybody back," he hollered as he flipped the deadbolt.

Everyone shuffled a few steps back, but not so far they couldn't watch Carl's twisty–turny approach as he stumbled across the gravel parking lot. He held the shotgun's butt while the long barrel of the business end bounced against the pavement as he lugged it behind him. Even from this distance, she couldn't miss that he was two drinks beyond drunk.

The operator answered on the second ring. "Salvation 911, please state your emergency."

"Carl Brennan is outside the Sweet Salvation Brewery with a shotgun. He's drunk."

"Is everyone okay?" the operator asked in a no-nonsense voice.

Natalie glanced around at the staff who'd inched closed to the window, despite Sean glowering at them from the door. "Yes."

In a town where most folks had fired a gun by the time their age hit double digits, just the sight of a shotgun wasn't going to make them twitch in fear. That and the fact that everyone in town would be talking about nothing else but this for the next few weeks at least had them glued to the glass. The staff would be getting free drinks at the Boot Scoot Boogie all night for telling this tale.

"Good. You said he has a gun?" the operator asked.

"Yeah." She blinked rapidly in surprise as Carl gave someone only he could see a big hug and then started kissing the air. *What the hell?*

"What kind of gun is it?"

Natalie stepped around the bar and strode over to the door. Sean sidestepped to stand in front of her and block her body from being a target, but not before she noticed the orange tip on the end of the shotgun. Since she'd gotten a similar firearm for her tenth birthday, she knew exactly what the orange meant.

"You've got to be kidding me." Natalie ground her teeth practically to dust. Of all the stupid things in the world. Carl had brought a damn toy BB gun to a brewery fight.

"What's happening?" The operator's tone sharpened.

Natalie shook her head in disbelief. "It's a BB gun, not a shotgun."

"You sure?" Sean whispered out of the side of his mouth.

"Trust me, no one from Salvation would mistake that." She jerked her head toward the staff, who looked about as scared as a dog napping in the sun. "Why do you think they're all close enough to fog up the window?"

"Ma'am." The operator broke up the conversation. "Is he threatening anyone with it?"

Trying—and failing—to keep the annoyance out of her voice, Natalie answered, "You don't call bringing a gun—even a BB gun—to your former place of employment threatening?"

"Ma'am," the operator said, speaking in the soothing tone used universally by kindergarten teachers that grated down Natalie's spine. "I understand your point, but I need to let the deputies on their way know if the suspect is pointing a gun at anyone."

As much as it pained her, she had to admit it was a valid inquiry. Natalie craned her neck around Sean's bulk to get a better look.

Carl stood in the middle of the parking lot, staring at the cloudless winter sky, a look of absolute Zen on his normally surly face...

She held the phone receiver away from her ear and strained to hear...

Yep, he was singing.

"No, he's not threatening anyone." She sighed. God, did nothing normal ever happen in Salvation? "He's singing."

"Singing?" The operator's voice went up an octave.

"Classic rock." Sean muttered. "Maybe Nirvana."

"Are you sure he's singing?" the operator asked, surprise making her voice crack. "I know Carl Brennan. I've seen him drunk and in lockup plenty of times. I've never seen him singing. Usually he's as mean as a teenage girl cut off from her cell phone"

"You're missing out then," Natalie responded. "He's actually better than the last cover band they had at the Boot Scoot Boogie."

"I was there. That's not saying much." The operator chuckled.

The ends of Natalie's lips twitched in a smile when Carl jackknifed at the waist. He started making herky–jerky motions as his cheeks puffed out. After a few deep breaths he straightened, hiccuped, and finished with a woozy smile before giving a quick salute to the Sweet Salvation Brewery sign. A second later he waved around like an inflatable dancing man at a car lot...and then threw up.

The brewery staff let out a collective "ewwwww" and took a step back. It seemed that the possibility of getting shot wasn't worth losing a good seat. But puke? Everyone hop–stepped it away. Natalie rolled her eyes. The whole town was cracked in the head.

Carl stripped off his coat and started wiping down the sign, but the arm holding the shotgun got tangled up in a sleeve. He tried to jerk it free. The move threw him off balance and he tumbled over. He hit the ground and a shot went off.

Everyone in the brewery's tasting room froze.

"Ma'am, I heard a shot. Is everyone okay?"

A small red stain bloomed on Carl's sleeve, right above his elbow. He clutched his arm and twisted the ground. The BB gun lay a few feet away from where he'd fallen.

Her mind was six steps ahead before she'd even whipped around and ran back to the bar. "You'd better get an ambulance out here. Carl shot himself."

"The deputies are a few minutes out, ma'am."

She rounded the bar and raced to the supplies. Carl was an ass, and she had to admit a part of her enjoyed seeing him in pain after all he'd done, but she couldn't leave him out there to bleed to death. BB guns weren't usually dangerous, but you clip a major vein or artery and that was all she wrote. "Hailey, take this." She handed the phone to the brewery's office manager, grabbed a handful of souvenir Sweet Salvation Brewery T–shirts and towels, and sprinted to the door.

"Oh no." Sean blocked her path.

She pushed against the immovable arm keeping her from walking out the brewery's front door. "He's drunk, not dangerous."

"And you think the two are mutually exclusive?" The low growl in his voice had nothing on the ice in his eyes. Whatever he'd seen in his life before he got to Salvation must have taught him the truth of that lesson with brutal efficiency.

But life had taught her things too. The main one being you couldn't run away from all the ugly in the world, sometimes you had to face it and tell it to fuck off.

"I'm not leaving a man in agony on the front lawn." She dipped underneath his arm and pushed open the door.

Sean muttered a curse and followed her into the sunshine. "He's not dying." He grabbed her arm, yanking her to a stop.

"You a doctor all of a sudden?" She shoved his hand away, spun on a heel, and hustled to the injured Carl.

Short of hauling Natalie screaming back into the brewery, there wasn't a damn thing Sean could do to stop her from helping Carl, who was sweating like an ice cube at the beach and taking in shallow breaths. The pain, however, didn't seem to be having any effect on Carl's attitude. If it wasn't for the blood, Sean would have thought the idiot had shot at himself and missed.

True to form, Natalie had gotten the old brewmaster's sleeve up enough to expose the BB gun wound and its messy aftermath. Sean may have played the hero on the big screen, but without a stunt double and a screenwriter, he was just fumbling out in the wind.

But not Natalie.

Even as Sean plotted how to get her back into the brewery before the pain sobered Carl up and he roared back into his normal mean–ass self, Sean admired the confidence it took for Natalie to do the right thing, even when it could come back and bite her on the ass. Not a lot of people did that anymore. Hell, the vast majority of people didn't do that anymore.

Natalie jerked Sean down until the gravel pebbles bit into his knees. "Hold this." She pressed his hand hard against the fast–bleeding wound in Carl's upper arm.

She rolled back on her heels and eyeballed the wound. "Damn it, Carl, that thing is bleeding like crazy. Did you use a pointed pellet?"

"What difference does that make?" Sean asked over the wailing of the sirens.

The sheriff's deputies were close enough now that he could see the cherry tops barreling down the road. His nerves jangled. For the past few years he'd done everything in his power to avoid law enforcement. His fake driver's license was good enough for a casual glance, but one quick call to check it out and the jig was up.

"Those are the best pellets for hunting small game. They're accurate as all get out and can do some real damage." She raised Carl's arm up above his head. "Keep tight pressure on the wound. We don't want him to lose too much blood before the paramedics take over."

"Well, aren't you shweet." Carl giggled at his own joke then winced at the pain it must have caused when he shook his injured arm. "A Shweet that's shweet."

Sean increased the pressure on the other man's wounds. A little reminder to be polite? Maybe. "You're drunk."

Two cruisers and an ambulance sped into the lot, spitting out gravel from beneath the tread of their tires.

Carl didn't even twitch despite the weight bearing down on him, instead he shook his head in slow motion like a stoned surfer. "Haven't had a shingle drink." His gaze flicked up and down repeatedly. Not as though he was really looking at or for anyone, but as if he couldn't help it.

Natalie snorted.

The cold wind carried the sound of the cruisers' doors slamming shut to where they huddled in the brewery sign's shadow.

"Really." Carl struggled to sit up with more force than expected from someone who was out of it enough to try to make out with an invisible person.

If he wasn't drunk, the dude was on something.

Sean used his free hand to press down on Carl's shoulder, stilling him, and tried to figure out what the fuck was going on. Carl's pupils were huge, but he'd never been a user that Sean had noticed or heard gossip about. In the past when the old brewmaster had been on a bender, not an unusual occurrence, he'd reeked of cheap bourbon. Sean took in a deep breath.

Carl could use a shower but that was it.

Unease zapped Sean like static electricity. "That doesn't explain why you're here with a gun. What were you planning to fuck up today? Or were you just going to shoot up the brewery?"

Natalie shifted beside him, drawing his attention. Standing straight and proud with a determined tilt to her chin, she stared not at Carl but at Sean with a quiet fierceness. She nodded her head. Carl may hate both of them, but if Sean could just get the former brewmaster to confess. Her strength and confidence in him floored him. He didn't doubt for a second that she wanted to tear Carl apart bone by bone, but something held her back. Maybe the same thing eating away at the back of his brain.

"What the fuck you talkin' about, boy?" Carl snarled. "This ish my brewery. Anybody messes with it and I'll kick their ass six ways to Shunday." He squinted up at them as the paramedics hustled across the lot. "Lemme go. I've got beer to brew."

"Maybe somewhere, but not here." The possibilities rumbled through his mind. Carl had to be high, but on what? Sean scooted aside so the taller of the two paramedics could take over, but maintained his hold on Carl's shoulders. As long as Natalie was around, he wasn't letting this asshole off the ground. "He's on something."

"Fuck you, boy." Outrage turned Carl's face a deep red. "I don't do drugs."

And movie popcorn isn't overpriced. Sean rolled his eyes.

The action had Carl sputtering in rage and he jackknifed into a sitting position, then broke out of Sean's grasp and sent the paramedic sprawling to the ground before the bleeding man scrambling to his feet. His injured arm hung limp at his side and a trickle of blood rushed down his forearm. Not that Carl seemed to notice or care.

Ignoring Sean, Carl laser–beamed him attention on Natalie. "You interfering bitch."

He lunged toward her.

The sound of footsteps rushing toward them registered, but Sean knew they wouldn't get to them in time. Acting on instinct, he barreled forward, intent on crushing Carl before the man reached Natalie.

He'd spent his formative years learning how to fight from stuntmen on the set, skills he'd found practical use for when he got older and finally stood up to his father.

His shoulder connected with Carl's stomach and he wrapped his arms around the man's paunchy middle and pushed forward. The momentum of his attack knocked Carl on his ass. Sean landed on top of him, letting his full weight pin the former brewmaster to the gravel parking lot.

Rage twisted Carl's face into an almost animalistic expression of pure hatred. "I know all about you," he bellowed as he managed to get his shoulders up off the ground. "Don't think I don't."

Sean clamped onto Carl's bony shoulders and shoved him back down. "Shut it, Brennan."

"From your name to your qualifications, you're nothing but a fraud." Spittle gathered at the corners of his mouth because of the force of his words. "You're as phony as a three dollar bill and you know it."

Carl had tipped off Rupert. He must have. How Carl had discovered the truth didn't matter, but the clock was ticking on Sean's time in Salvation.

Two deputies and the other paramedic appeared in Sean's periphery vision before they moved in closer and took over holding Carl down.

"You." The paramedic nodded at Sean. "Mosey on back. We got him now. Anyway, the deputies want to take your statement. Yours too, Ms. Sweet."

They'd made it about a few yards away when Natalie pulled him to the side. "What in the hell was that about?"

Reaching deep for his rusty acting skills, Sean forced the tension out of his shoulders and let his face relax into a neutral mask. "The guy's out of his mind."

"No argument there." She eyed him suspiciously. "But there's something to it, isn't there?"

For half a second the truth balanced on the tip of his tongue, and with it, a redemption he hadn't realized he'd wanted. He hadn't trusted anyone with his real identity, not since he'd hot–wired that car and drove until the Hollywood sign was only a vague memory. Not for the millions he'd left in a bank account. Not for the easy fame and even easier women. Not for the family who'd only seen him as a paycheck. But Natalie....

Looking into her crystal–clear blue eyes half hidden behind the black–framed glasses, he couldn't help but believe she'd understand why he'd done it.

"Howdy folks. Looks like you've had some excitement around here." Gravel crunched under the deputy's rubber–soled boots as he approached. He stopped beside them and withdrew a notepad from his shirt pocket. "Let's get started with some names."

Always quick on her feet, it only took a second for Natalie to refocus on the deputy. "Natalie Sweet."

"That one I knew. You're kind of hard to miss around town." The flirting tone in the deputy's voice and the way he leaned toward Natalie set Sean's teeth on edge. "How about you?"

"Sean." The word came out as half a threat.

The deputy straightened and hardened his jaw. "Gotta last name, Sean?"

More than one. "O'Dell." He rubbed the back of his neck and realized just how damn sick of lying he'd become.

"Okay then." The deputy flipped open the small notepad. "Why don't you start at the beginning and walk me through what just went down."

Chapter Eleven

The day after paramedics hauled a ranting Carl into the ambulance, a sense of impending doom continued to stalk Natalie like a hunter closing in on a deer. To counteract the uncertainty, she fell into her normal routine at the brewery with a vengeance. She poured one–hundred–and–forty–five–degree water into her cup of loose leaf Gyokuro green tea at exactly five after eight. Next, she powered up her laptop and tuned into an internet ambient–music station. After two minutes of calming music, she removed the tea infuser, set it aside, and inhaled the flowery–green aroma.

Normally, this was all it took to put her back on an even keel, but the ghost of anxiety still skittered across the back of her neck, setting her hair on end. Today she might need a double shot of teatime Zen—or another session with Sean in the reference room. She could blame it on the sex, but the feeling making her stomach do the loop–de–loop whenever she thought of Sean had nothing to do with sex—although that sure as hell wasn't anything to scoff at.

The memory pulled her lips into a smile. Always tied to propriety, she hadn't ever done it outside of a bed. Oh, she'd done a hell of a lot *in* that bed, but yesterday was a first in more than one way.

"So did you hear?"

Natalie jumped at her sister's voice, sending the green tea sloshing around inside her cup and tweaking her apprehension levels up five notches. "Ever hear of knocking?"

"Jumpy, sis?" Miranda strolled in, holding a paper bag in her outstretched hands. "I come baring double–chocolate donuts from the Heaven Sent Bakery."

Her mouth watered. The donuts were an explosion of chocolate goodness with even more chocolate on top. Eating one was almost as good as a bookshelf organized by genre and alphabetized by the authors' last names.

"I could use a couple decades of quiet and calm." Natalie snagged the bag. "But this will do."

"I'm so sorry." Miranda sank into the guest chair, her shoulders slumped. "I never thought when I conned you into coming down that it would be like this. I know Olivia and I kid you about the pearls and your lists, but it comes from a place of love. We're both really proud of how far you've come."

Warmth washed over her, that one–of–a–kind sisterly love of knowing someone was in her corner. After her breakdown during college, her sisters could have treated her like a broken doll that had been carelessly glued back together. But they hadn't, and for that she'd be eternally grateful. Bald lies in the face of an ugly truth never sat well with her. She'd have shattered under kid gloves, and thanks to their tough love, she'd found the strength she'd thought she'd lost.

"That makes three of us." She saluted Miranda with a donut. "The fact that I haven't had a knee–knocking anxiety attack despite all of this crazy is comforting."

Her sister grinned and grabbed the remaining donut. "You're a hell of a lot tougher than you look."

"You know I look just like you." Mirror reflections, at least on the outside. But on the inside? What she wouldn't give for Miranda's bone–deep confidence, or Olivia's willingness to take chances, instead of being the Nervous Nelly middle sister.

Miranda laughed. "Touché."

Needing to pull her thoughts away from the maudlin edge, Natalie turned the conversation back to what had brought her sister into the office in the first place. "Enough touchy–feely sisterly love, what gossip did you just hear?"

Miranda held up her pointer finger and finished her mouthful of donut. "Well, Logan and Hud were having lunch at The Kitchen Sink today when the sheriff came in for pie."

"Fascinating." She polished off her own donut. "Your fiancé and his best friend were eating and saw someone go to The Kitchen Sink for pie? Well, I never."

"Oh, shut up." Miranda flung a donut chunk at her. "Well, Ruby Sue put the screws to the sheriff. He told her that Carl tested positive for PCP, which would explain the paranoid delusions and general violent whack–a–do–ness from the other day. We're lucky he only had a BB gun with him. People go nuts on that stuff."

Natalie scooped her jaw up off the floor. "Damn."

"Exactly." She leaned forward, elbows on her knees, and dropped her voice to a whisper. "Supposedly there wasn't very much in his system."

"And the sheriff just spilled all of that?" Natalie contemplated the few bits of loose tea floating in her cup.

"Do you know of anyone who can withstand Ruby Sue's interrogations?"

She considered it, trying to recall a single instance of that happening, and came up with nothing. "Nope."

"That's where the good news ends."

With care, she set her cup down on a coaster. She doubted green tea was going to be enough to smooth over whatever was coming next. "That was good news?"

"Pretty much." Miranda sighed. "I just got off the phone with the sheriff's investigator assigned to our case," Miranda continued. "While he admits Carl is the likely suspect *if*—and he stressed that—anything nefarious happened, there's no physical proof to tie him to the possible sabotage, and there's not much more they can do."

Of course not. Old habits died hard in Salvation, and treating the Sweets like the redheaded stepchildren had become second nature to the people who'd lived there over the past hundred years.

"Great." She traced the length of her pearl necklace. "So now we just keep our eyes open and move forward with brewery operations?"

Miranda shrugged. "Pretty much."

"Right back at the beginning."

"Not completely." Miranda's body language was nonchalant, but Natalie knew better than most when her sister was going in for the kill. "After Ruby Sue got done with the sheriff, she turned her laser beam of truth on Logan and Hud."

"Looking for wedding details?" *Please say yes.*

"Nope." Miranda shook her head. "She wanted to know all about you and Sean."

Her stomach dive–bombed to her knees. "Great." She traced the length of her pearl necklace. Salvation's gossip gods giveth and they taketh away. "What did they tell her?"

Miranda shrugged. "Not much they could tell. It's not like there's anything going on."

One pearl. Two pearl. Three pearl. "Exactly."

"Of course not, because you'd totally tell your big sister if there was," Miranda said. "From what I hear, you and Sean made quite the team when Carl showed up. Maybe you two should...work together more often."

Oh no, she wasn't taking that bait. She wasn't sure exactly what she was doing with Sean but it scared her just as much as it thrilled her. "I'll keep that in mind."

Had someone heard them? Then she remembered how Hailey had burst into the room as soon as their clothes were back on. Had she been outside the whole time, trying to get their attention, but they'd been too focused on each other to hear the outside world? Natalie's cheeks burned. She was falling back onto old habits. Sex with the unobtainable—in this case an employee—when what she needed was to find someone with relationship potential.

Miranda arched her eyebrows and cocked her head to the side. "Oh, if Olivia could see you now, you'd be in so much trouble."

Too late for that. Natalie was already neck deep in it.

Natalie paused outside of Sean's closed office door and took a deep breath. She'd just talk to him. Work only. No mind–melting kisses. No sexual tension. No noticing his amazing ass that you could bounce a quarter off of. Definitely no sex. She wasn't sure she could take a second time without getting her heart broken—and that was *not* part of her master plan to have a healthy, non–compartmentalized relationship.

Plan. Brewery. Keep it together, Natalie.

Miranda was right. To implement the changes, she had to get the staff's buy in, and to do that, she needed Sean. She wouldn't even notice his broad shoulders or the way he chewed his bottom lip when he rolled a problem around in his head.

She could do this.

She *would* do this.

So why are you standing here with your hand hovering in the air, unable to knock on his door?

Straightening her shoulders and snapping on an imaginary chastity belt, she rapped her knuckles against the wood.

"It's open." Sean's deep voice stirred up nothing but trouble inside her.

Steeling her nerve, she turned the knob and walked in. "Hey, do you have a minute?"

Sean looked up from the notes he was writing in his cramped script. He'd tossed his Sweet Salvation Brewery hat on top of the file cabinet, leaving his chin–length waves loose and wild. Like him. God, that enough should make her control freak self–padlock her knees together. If only her libido worked that way.

She clutched her clipboard closer to her chest.

His gaze zeroed in on it, and his pupils dilated and darkened. "I don't know." A slow, deadly smile curled his lips, and he relaxed back against his chair. "You've got that clipboard and too many clothes on."

"Very funny." Heat blazed against her cheeks. "Look. I've been thinking."

"That's always trouble." His flirtatious tone remained, but his body sharpened as he leaned forward, tension thrumming off him.

Her breath caught and she almost stumbled back. Everything about him screamed danger. To her heart. To her sanity. To her ability to control the chaos. Tightening her grip on the clipboard, she squeezed it close to her chest like a shield.

"Yesterday shouldn't have happened. People are already talking—neither of us wants that. We don't need to pretend it was anything more than temporary insanity."

That last bit was harder to get out than she'd expected. Each word slashed against her skin like a whip, leaving a red, raw welt in its wake.

"Who said I was pretending?" The deadly serious look in his brown eyes made her heart stutter. "I sure as hell hope you weren't."

"Oh." For once, it was Natalie who didn't have a thing to say, because he was right. She hadn't been pretending at all. She wasn't falling for her brewmaster—she already had.

He shrugged and rubbed his palm against his head. God, she could still feel the smoothness of his hair as she'd run her fingers through it while he'd licked her nipples. A slow and easy warmth invaded her body.

Remember the plan, Natalie.

Latching on to her logical side before lust could tip its hand, Natalie shot him a dirty look and remained standing to hold on to the height advantage. "Enough procrastinating. We need to get these changes in place." She whipped a copy of her plan from the clipboard. Back in control of her libido—okay, barely, but it was still control—her hand didn't even shake.

Not much anyway.

He glanced down at the papers but didn't take them. "Why?"

Natalie took a deep breath, resisting the urge to roll up the paper and smack him in the head. Instead, she rounded the desk, stopped on the edge of his hot–guy–pheromone force field and slapped the papers down in the middle of his desk.

"Because the brewery has so much potential." She dropped her clipboard to the desk, the clatter of it hitting the wood echoing her own frustration. "My sisters and I own this brewery, we know what needs to be done to make it better, and it's past time you got on board."

Power streamed through her veins, revving her up from the inside out. She might have her faults, but her belief in what the right processes could do to improve efficiency wasn't one of them. If only that strategy worked as well in her relationships as it did in business.

Sean rolled back from the desk, interlocked his fingers, and rested them on top of his head. "Is it so wrong to just let it be?"

"Yeah, it is."

Just let it be?

If she just let things be, she never would have reenrolled in college after dropping out, never would have found a healthy outlet for her anxiety, and never would have made good on what right now seemed like an insane promise to stop compartmentalizing sex and relationships.

Let it be.

Total crazy talk.

"Why just be okay when you can be more?"

He stiffened in his seat, and something dark flashed in his brown eyes. "So nothing but the best at any cost, huh?"

Just the way he said it, with such a cold, hard tone, sent a chill down her spine. Knowing she was treading on thin ice but not understanding why, she took a half step back and let out a cleansing breath. She'd sold more stubborn people than Sean on her ideas before. She could do it now.

"Not exactly." Slowly, she slid the printout of her plan across the desk. "Take a look. You'll see the changes are about improving efficiency and strengthening our production abilities."

He stared at the papers but didn't reach out to take them. "Part of what makes the Sweet Salvation Brewery special is the way we make our beer with care and commitment. It's who we are."

"Instead of thinking only the worst, why don't you at least take a look?"

"You and your sisters own the place," he snapped. "Why not just change everything by fiat?"

She considered it. It had happened at other businesses. Management had accepted her recommendations and told underlings it was this way or the highway. The results had always been tainted by the ensuing turnover and bitterness. The total brewery staff clocked in at twenty–five, many of whom had been there since the Sweet triplets were in middle school. Even a small change, if it wasn't supported by key team members, could negatively affect the whole process and alienate the staff.

So why not just change everything by fiat?

"Because it's not our style." She shrugged and sat down on the corner of his desk. "We want your buy in."

"What about you?" He dropped his arms and rolled his chair closer so that his knees almost touched her legs dangling from his desk. "What do you want?"

Electricity zapped between them, and she nearly fell into his deep–brown eyes—not to mention his lap.

Fighting to maintain proper decorum, she tapped the papers on his desk. "This is what I want."

"No." Sean leaned forward, his knee brushing against her leg. "What do you really want?"

Only his jeans and her winter tights kept them from skin–to–skin contact, but it wasn't enough to keep her from going jittery and molten at once. Who was she kidding? A three–foot steel wall probably wouldn't be enough for her not to notice him. The man was fast becoming her kryptonite.

She should move—but she didn't.

"I don't think this is an appropriate conversation for employer and employee."

"It wouldn't be the first time we were inappropriate." He winked and scooted closer. Now his legs bracketed hers, and his palms rested flat on the desk, one on either side of her hips. "Did you forget yesterday? I haven't."

"You're just trying to throw me off my game." That came out way too breathy. What was it about this man that made her lose control so easily?

Sean rose from this chair but kept his hands planted on the desk. Leaning forward, he didn't stop until his lips were millimeters from her ear. "Is it working?" he asked in a teasing growl.

Hell yes. "No."

He chuckled. "Really?"

Low and rumbly, his single–word question sent desire spiraling through her like a tornado of want and need and gimmie–some–of–that–hottie–now desire. But everything was so new, she didn't have enough data to understand what was going on. There wasn't a flowchart for how to act when you'd fallen for an employee. So she scrambled to safer conversational ground.

"Really." She pushed him away and stood before her lust overwhelmed her ability to breathe and think straight, her knees a little shakier than she wanted to admit even to herself, and delivered a pointed stare at his arm blocking her retreat.

He took a few steps back to give her room to escape. And that's what it was; they both knew it.

"Read it." She grabbed her clipboard from the desk and held it close. "After all, I was right about organizing your office."

He glanced around at his still–clean office before giving her a half–smile that melted everything south of her waist and made her rethink the importance of oxygen. "One condition."

Her heart tripped over itself and banged against her ribs. Her lips parted. "What's that?"

"Research the Southeast Brewers Invitational and what it can do for a brewery's reputation." He snagged a brochure from his top drawer and handed it to her. "That's where we need to be concentrating. Winning could make the Sweet Salvation Brewery."

She took it, careful to keep her fingers from brushing his, and backpedaled to the office door. A girl could only take so much temptation after all. "That may be true, but it won't mean a damn thing if we can't fill the orders without breaking the bank."

"So you think the artist of alcohol and the organizational queen can work together?" Sean asked.

With the length of the office between them, Natalie regained her natural balance. Mostly. "Something like that."

His phone buzzed. "Yeah?" He paused. "Sure, she's right here."

She took the phone and the air sizzled around them when her fingers brushed his. "Hello?"

"Natalie, there's a guy here to see you," Hailey said. "His name is Rupert Crowley."

Fingers crossed it was the new hops and barley dealer here to negotiate next year's prices. "Send him to my office. I'll be there in a minute."

"You got it."

Natalie hung up the phone. "I have to go."

Sean tipped an imaginary hat at her. "Looking forward to talking again soon."

Damn her mutinous body, so was she.

Sean finished the last page of Natalie's twenty–five–point plan, dropped it on his desk and sat back. The woman was scary smart and damn good at her job. The changes she outlined seemed so obvious and a hell of a lot less crazy once he'd read them in black and white. He rubbed the back of his neck hard enough to heat his palm, but not enough to wipe out the memory of the lengths he'd gone to avoid even taking a look at Natalie's plan.

And the asshat of the year award goes to...me.

It really sucked that he couldn't even cook something as simple as popcorn, because he was going to be eating crow for days.

He pushed away from the desk and stood. Better to get it over with sooner rather than later. Anyway, it wasn't as if he was making any headway on creating a unique new stout recipe. Everything he'd come up with in the past two days had lacked any kind of punch. He glanced down at the notes he'd scrawled in the notebook laying open in the middle of his clean desk.

One word was circled: cherry.

It wasn't unheard of for cherry to be in beer. The cherry lambic was made by fermenting the lambic with sour Morello cherries. Maybe Natalie had something.

Again.

With traditional ales and lagers, the fermentation was carefully controlled and included specific cultivated strains of brewer's yeast. But a lambic utilized spontaneous fermentation with wild yeast and bacteria from Brussels. If he could apply some of the lambic process to the stout, he could create a unique sweet and sour stout that would stand out at the Southeast Brewers Invitational.

He turned the idea over in his head, trying to think around the mental image of Natalie in the reference room and the way her pink lips had moved when she'd said the word cherry. In a heartbeat, he was back in that tiny room, surrounded by the honeysuckle scent that clung to her tightly bound hair. He'd stood close enough that, with the slightest movement, he could have reached out and touched her soft skin hidden beneath the naughty librarian cardigan and sensible skirt.

His fingers itched to touch her now.

As much as she'd driven him to distraction when she'd arrived at the brewery with her clipboard and no–nonsense attitude, he hadn't stopped thinking about her since the first time she'd said "flowchart". The pull only gained strength the more time he spent with her. Shit, their meeting in his office this afternoon had left him with a hard–on big enough to leave a zipper imprint on his dick.

She felt it too, he knew it, but propriety and office etiquette held her back from thinking it could be more. He wished he had as good of an excuse. Lying through his teeth about who he was and why he was in Salvation didn't tread the same moral high ground. Either way, she was off limits.

Well, to paraphrase Bogie, his personal problems didn't amount to a hill of beans in this crazy world, so he might as well man up and take on something he could fix: the brewery. Swiping Natalie's plan off his desk, he stood and hustled out into the hallway, intent on finding the world's sexiest efficiency expert.

And for a man about to scarf down a large slice of humble pie, he was pretty damn happy about it.

"Yo, Sean." Billy poked his head through the swinging door separating the offices from the brewery floor. Today was his first day back and, except for the bandage covering a buttload of stitches on his forehead, he looked no worse for the wear. "Come check this out."

Indecision tugged at Sean. The need to go see Natalie had him strung tight, but he couldn't exactly put off Billy when the kid had taken one for the team practically right between the eyes. "Whatcha got?"

His gaze dropped to the ground and he gulped. "The delivery trucks all have flat tires."

"Are you fucking kidding me?" Carl was still in jail, of this he had no doubt. The judge had been plenty pissed at the former brewmaster and had revoked his bond. Maybe Billy was still suffering from the head injury and had misunderstood what he'd seen? Yeah, because that was likely. "All of them?"

"Yep." The kid's eyes were clear and focused. "Saw it myself."

He shoved the brim of his Sweet Salvation Brewery baseball hat lower on his forehead. "Fuck me running."

"No thank you." Billy grinned.

Sean flipped him off. "Smart ass. Come on."

They hustled through the brewery and out the open loading dock door. Sweet Salvation Brewery had built up their delivery fleet to three trucks, each one of which was parked behind the building. As he stormed toward them, he could see they had sunken down to the rims.

One tire he could understand, but multiple tires on each of the vehicles? That wasn't an accident, and someone was going to pay, even if Sean had to deliver justice himself. "Call the sheriff's office."

"You got it." Billy took off back inside the brewery.

An angry heat seared him from the toes up, and if he'd looked in a mirror at that moment, he wouldn't have been surprised to see a twisted, red–faced, bearded, younger version of his father staring back at him.

Alone in the gathering twilight, Sean crisscrossed the gravel rear parking lot, the blood pounding in his ears with every determined step. The security lights clicked on and he spun around.

Billy stood by the switch, the phone to his ear.

Sean waved a hand. "Thanks."

After getting a thumbs–up from Billy, he turned back to his perusal. A sparkle amid the dusty gray gravel grabbed his attention. He squatted down and picked up the tiny piece of metal.

A nail.

Everything inside him went still, cold, and quiet. Whoever had it in for the brewery wasn't done wreaking havoc. He glanced back at Billy and his bandaged head. The kid could have been killed or seriously injured. If the truck tires hadn't lost air pressure so fast in the cool winter air, the nails would have stayed embedded in the tread until the drivers had a blowout while going seventy miles an hour on the highway. He tossed the nail into a bin.

At that moment, he understood better than he ever had in his life the kind of rage that had torn his dad up inside. He looked around and the ground resembled a disco ball, with little silver nails scattered everywhere. “Dammit.”

It only took a few minutes to confirm the same nail circle surrounded the other trucks’ tires. Someone was fucking with the brewery, and they were done trying to hide it.

Good. That would just make finding the asshole easier.

Chapter Twelve

The photo shook in Natalie's hand as she sat behind her desk. It had been torn it from an old copy of *People* magazine. The man pictured had to be in his early twenties. Brown, short hair artfully tousled, a surfer's tan, and brown eyes that kicked her pulse into overdrive even when the man in question wasn't within touching distance. And, of course, the thin scar just above one eyebrow.

Sean, *her Sean*, wasn't Sean O'Dell at all.

The missing paperwork.

The W–2 he still hadn't completed.

The way he never talked about family or his past or about anything much at all.

Her stomach sank under the weight of the realization, and she reached for her talisman. The round pearls felt warm to the touch as her fingertips slid up and down the strand around her neck.

She glanced at the clock. Only an hour ago, everything had been right with the world. And then Rupert Crowley with *Hollywood and Vines Reports* had strolled into her office and turned everything upside down faster than a tsunami.

"This can't be right." Her voice shook and she pushed the photo across her desk.

The reporter sitting across from her reclaimed the photo and slid it into a manila folder. "I'm afraid, Ms. Sweet, it is."

Her fingers danced across her pearl necklace as her brain scrambled to put the pieces together, to force the story to make sense.

Sean was a movie star. Not just that, he'd been a damn good one. His face had been on the front of most major papers when he'd disappeared. Some said drug overdose. Others speculated he'd lost his mind. *The American Inquirer* even had a report that he'd been the *Misery*–style victim of an overzealous female fan.

In reality, he'd ended up as the brewmaster at a small brewery in Virginia. Yeah, it was going to take a while to make that fit under the "logical category" heading on a chart.

Fake sincerity clung to Rupert Crowley like cheap cologne as he watched her, no doubt mentally recording her every reaction. It took everything she had not to choke on the figurative stench. "There may be some resemblance."

"Not *some* resemblance," he insisted. "Sean O'Dell *is* Sean Duvin."

Despite what her brain knew to be true, part of her couldn't accept it. The Sean she knew would never lie about something like this. "You don't—"

"Please, Ms. Sweet, I appreciate your loyalty to your employees, but I've been chasing this story for years. I'm not going to give up now."

And he wouldn't. The reporter practically hummed with fanatical determination.

"Why are you so intent on finding him?" Maybe if he left, they could go back to before. She could pretend this whole conversation never took place. The early stages of an anxiety attack pinched her lungs and she picked up the pace of her fingers traveling over the pearls.

"I'm a reporter. I chase the stories that interest my readers and with the new live webstream, viewers. And, for better or worse, they are fascinated by the disappearance of one of Hollywood's hottest actors at the peak of his popularity. Imagine, if you would, Ms. Sweet, if LeBron James vanished, never to be heard from again. Even non–basketball fans would be curious about what had happened to one of the greatest players of all time and why he went into hiding."

"So that's what this is for you, a story?" Natalie divided her attention between his answer and maintaining slow, steady breaths, just like Dr. Kenning had taught her.

"In the beginning, I suppose it was." Rupert leaned forward, an excited gleam in his eyes. He was in full storytelling mode and obviously enjoyed it. "It really is an amazing story. Sean started out as a child actor on kids' shows and commercials, working steadily for years without any hint of trouble. Then he became a teenager and things got a little sketchy. Drugs, alcohol, and women were all easy to get for a teen heartthrob with a devoted following. If Tumblr had been as hot then as it is now, he would have been its biggest draw. Of course, that kind of life catches up with a boy. He showed up late to the set, refused to attend the mandated educational classes, and needed extra time in makeup to cover the results of his carousing. Directors and producers lost patience with him, and it looked as if he was going to be another Hollywood tragedy."

Despite herself, Natalie was sucked into the tale. "What changed?"

"Oh yes, the third act." Rupert rubbed his supernaturally tanned hands together. "So he shows up for an audition to play a dying teenager in a made–for–TV movie. He blows the casting people away, but he has this reputation following him, so they don't want to hire him. In the end, they decide to take a chance. He won a Golden Globe for that part. More critically acclaimed performances followed in movies and TV until, only a few short years later, he was accepting an Oscar for best supporting actor. Then—*poof!*—he disappears."

Rupert sat back in his chair, a self–satisfied, snarky twist to his thin lips.

Knee jiggling under the desk, Natalie reached for her cup in an effort to buy time for the deafening static in her head to fade back into the background. She couldn't go back to that anxious place, not now. She took a slow, measured sip of green tea that had cooled long ago. The liquid did nothing to relieve her thirst or calm her churning stomach.

"Are you all right, Ms. Sweet?" Rupert narrowed his gaze, giving her an assessing up and down.

The perusal was predatory, but not in a sexual way. No doubt the reporter was looking for cracks in her armor.

"I'm fine." She settled the cup on the saucer and clasped her hands in her lap. She inhaled. *Find a problem, fix a problem.* That was her mantra but this time, the problem had found her. She breathed out. "It sounds to me like he doesn't want to be found."

Rupert clapped his hands together. "Oh, but he doesn't have a choice in that, because I've found him. Americans love a redemption story. They instinctively root for the underdog. Sean Duvin is a story that combines both. He's the bad boy who made good when no one thought he had it in him."

The static grew in her head, threatening to drown out the rest of the world. She had to get the reporter out of her office, but not until she understood. "Why him?"

He tilted his head. "What do you mean, Ms. Sweet?"

"Don't be coy now." The urge to reach across her desk and strangle the slimeball was running neck and neck with the anxiety shrinking her lungs into the size of raisins. She thought of Sean—not the man Rupert had described, but the one she knew. The whole situation failed the logic test. "Why chase a man who obviously doesn't want to be found?"

He looked down and to the left before returning his gaze to her. "Let's say I'm personally invested. Not the wisest choice for a journalist, but it does happen." He flashed a blindingly white, insincere smile. "Finding Sean Duvin has become my life's mission. My sword in the stone, if you will, Ms. Sweet."

"And you see yourself as King Arthur?" The man's ego was big enough.

He paused and looked up at the ceiling, as if parsing the ancient legend's cast of characters. "More like Merlin, the man behind the scenes who makes everything work."

She sucked in a deep, cleansing breath, forcing her hands apart in her lap and flexing her fingers.

The tightness in her lungs lessened, and the static rolled back its volume.

"So what do you want with him?" Even though Sean had lied to her and everyone else at the brewery about who he was, there were few people she'd throw to a hyena like Crowley.

He shrugged his narrow shoulders. "What every reporter dreams about, an exclusive that will make their name."

Bingo. What a sleaze. Of course, the side benefit of his ridiculousness was the slow abatement of her anxiety. It was hard to get worked up over an idiot. "And I had assumed it was to satisfy your viewers' curiosity."

"Oh yes, of course. Who could forget the millions of viewers and readers who'd love to know what happened to their favorite, Ms. Sweet?"

Obviously Rupert Crowley. "You don't have concrete proof that our Sean is *your* Sean."

His barking laugh filled the room. "I'm going to let you in on a trade secret, my dear Ms. Sweet. When you're as close to your subject as I am, you don't need concrete proof. You just know."

"What even led you to Salvation?"

"The grace of God?" He laughed at his own joke. "Or in this case a tip from someone at the brewery."

"Carl Brennan?" That would explain the verbal swipes Carl had made at Sean the other day. She'd meant to follow up with him, but had gotten distracted. That seemed to happen a lot around Sean whenever she pressed him for answers.

He shifted in his seat. "I never reveal my sources."

"This whole conversation is ridiculous." She stood and walked around her desk toward the door. "I'll go get Sean and you'll see how wrong you are."

"No." His hand clapped around her wrist. "Not yet. And I'd appreciate it if you didn't mention our little conversation until I speak to him first. After all, if by some slim chance it's not the right Sean, well, there's no harm in keeping it our little secret."

She shook him off. "I don't think–"

"Twenty–four hours, Ms. Sweet." Desperation leaked into the words. "Can you give me that?"

Sean watched the deputy's cruiser disappear around the bend in the road connecting the Sweet Salvation Brewery to the main highway. As he'd suspected, Carl was cooling his heels in the county lockup without bail, which meant they were back to square one when it came to figuring out who was fucking with the brewery.

Looked like Natalie was going to get that late–night stakeout she'd planned. At least she already had a flowchart worked up for it. He grinned to himself. He may have run screaming from her clipboard before, but the damn thing with her different–colored pens had grown on him–just like Natalie.

Suddenly he couldn't wait to see her again and it had nothing to do with the brewery. Time to track his naughty librarian down. He yanked the door open and strode through the tasting room to the offices in back.

Without bothering to knock, Sean opened Natalie's door and strolled in. "We need to talk." He made it half a step before jamming to a stop.

Hailey stood behind Natalie's desk, her fingers on the computer keyboard. She jerked up and slapped a hand over her heart. "Sean!" She took in a shaky breath. "You scared me. With everything going on around here, you shouldn't be busting in on people."

"Sorry, I needed to talk to Natalie."

Hailey grinned. "What a coincidence, she's waiting for you in your office."

Couldn't wait to see him, huh? That was just the kind of good news he needed after the past hour. "Great." He pivoted and had one foot in the hallway when he pulled up short. "Can I help you with something?"

The office manager was already hunched back over Natalie's computer. "Unless you can perform magic and revive my printer from the dead, I'm stuck using Natalie's printer until the new one is delivered."

"Left my wand at home today."

"Isn't that always the case?" She shook her head. "By the way, what's going on with you and Natalie?"

Nothing. Everything. Something weird in–between that could turn into more. "Not sure."

"Better figure it out soon. I don't think she's the type who waits around." She hit a button on Natalie's keyboard and the printer hummed to life.

"Ain't that the truth?" He tipped his baseball cap and hustled down the hall to his office.

For the past fourteen minutes and thirty–three seconds, Natalie had ignored the papers laid willy–nilly on the filing cabinet, the two Styrofoam coffee cups stacked on the corner of Sean's desk and the copy of her twenty–five–point plan flipped over so only the back page showed. The longer she sat waiting, the more pissed she became, but what she needed to say had to be said behind closed doors. If she walked out that door she'd make a scene, and that couldn't happen.

She made plans and charts to avoid that ever happening again. Being in control wasn't just important, it was everything.

"Hey there." Sean strolled in, tension apparent in his high–perched shoulders, but some of it leaked out as he walked in and saw her.

Hers, on the other hand, ratcheted up. "Close the door."

"It's that kind of meeting, huh?" He raised his eyebrows and winked. The door clicked shut behind him.

Remaining in his chair, she crossed her arms and waited until he sat in his own guest chair. "Who are you?"

Sean's eyes rounded. "What do you mean?"

Natalie's heart dropped to her knees and she closed her eyes. A large part of her was hoping against logic that it wasn't true. That it had all been one crazy mistake. But it hadn't. She knew that now.

The static sounded in her ears, the white noise precursor to an uptick in her anxiety levels. Using all the powers of concentration she'd learned from Dr. Kenning and years of practicing yoga, she slowed her breathing and regained her equilibrium. If the situation hadn't been so damn depressing, she'd be celebrating the victory over her anxiety instead of wanting to cry.

Pushing all of the emotions she couldn't deal with at the moment into individualized compartments, she opened her eyes. "I had a visitor today named Rupert Crowley."

"Fuck." Sean swiped his baseball cap off his head and rammed his hands through his hair, revealing that telltale scar above his eyebrow.

"So it's true." An ache, deep and dark, twisted inside her.

He jumped up from the chair and paced from one end of the small office to the other. "What did he say?"

"Does it matter?" Needing something to do to keep her hands busy, she straightened the few items left out on his desk.

"Try to understand..." The plea in his voice reverberated across her most vulnerable places.

To fight it, she grabbed ahold of her anger with both hands, letting it lead her. "Who are you?"

A neutral mask, totally devoid of any expression had settled on his face and he stared at some spot over her left shoulder. "Sean Duvin."

Turning to face him, she asked the one question that thundered louder than all the others. "Why?"

"It's a long story. But I've been running for years and he found me anyway." He swept back his hair with one hand and shoved his hat back on, replacing his disguise.

But now that she'd seen the truth, she couldn't unsee the man behind the beard and the baseball hat. She noticed more too—like the pinched V between his eyes, the vein sticking out from his temple and the air of determined energy pulsing off him.

"Rupert Crowley is a sleazeball celebrity biographer and reporter." Sean practically growled the name. "He's made a small fortune writing stories speculating about whatever happened to Sean Duvin."

"I read one a few years ago. Not the biography, an article. Olivia was on the cover of *Chantal* magazine and there was an article about him—you—inside."

It hadn't been very flattering. Stories of Sean going missing for a day or two and then showing back up with mysterious bruises. Rumors about more women than one twenty–one–year–old man could handle. Grumblings about problems and drama with his family—lots of drama. None of which jived with the Sean she knew.

"I found out yesterday that he was in town and I almost ran again." He spoke quietly, but the underlying disappointment came through loud and clear. "But I couldn't."

The idea of him leaving shook her more than it should, especially considering what she had to do next. "Why didn't you?"

"This." Sean tapped a framed photo of the brewery hanging on the wall, his love for the place plain to see on his face. "I couldn't. I love this place. Your Uncle Julian, he saved me by taking a chance on me. I'd probably still be running if it wasn't for him. And you. There's a reason why I couldn't come up with the perfect stout recipe for the Southeast Brewers Invitational. I didn't understand the importance of mixing sweet in with the sour until I met you. I don't want to be anyone but the Sean O'Dell that I am around you."

Her shock evaporated under an angry blazing heat. He'd been lying to them. To her. For months. No wonder he kept his mouth shut so much. It was easier to keep track of the falsehoods that way.

What an idiot she'd been. She'd come back to Salvation to learn how to stop compartmentalizing her love life and had fallen for a guy who'd been doing it for his whole life. Wasn't that just her luck?

He reached out and tucked a loose strand of hair behind her ear, resting his palm against her cheek as if he couldn't stand to not touch her. "I could have run the minute Rupert Crowley called the brewery trying to find me. But I couldn't—still can't—leave *you*."

Anger. Confusion. Hurt. They all combined into the vicious brew swirling through her and she slapped his hand away.

"Of course not. How could you leave the boss you banged in the back of the brewery?" She shot up out of the chair. "You're working here with a fake social security number; that alone could get the brewery in major trouble. For claiming to care about it, you sure have a funny way of showing it."

"Your Uncle Julian and I worked out a deal," Sean confessed.

"Uncle Julian knew?" She wanted to pull her hair out in frustration. Of course Uncle Julian knew. The old coot had probably had a good laugh about screwing over Uncle Sam right good, never bothering to think about how much trouble the brewery could get into for knowingly working with someone using a fake identity.

That was it. Not a thing about the situation could be salvaged. It was over. Sean whatever-his-name–was had to get out. Natalie gave him wide berth and marched to the door.

"Please." He reached out and took her hands between his, the now familiar zing of attraction buzzing across her skin at his touch. "I hate to ask, but I need to be Sean O'Dell. Here. With you."

Natalie yanked her hand free. She wasn't about to make it that easy. "You've got to be kidding me. You want me to keep your secrets?"

"I know it's a lot to ask." He shook his head as if he still couldn't believe the truth had finally come out.

The brewery had enough shit dropping on it from above to add another problem to the mix. She was here to find solutions, not add to the problems.

"It's not a lot to ask. It's too much." She dropped her voice to a lower pitch and spoke in a slow and steady rhythm, despite her pulse's jerking jackrabbit speed. "Just pack up your stuff and get out."

"Natalie." Agony sliced through his words like a steel blade.

Of course it did. He was an Academy Award–winning actor, after all.

She turned the doorknob and pulled it open. "You're fired."

"What about yesterday? What about us?" He grabbed her hand and yanked her to his broad chest before leaning down for a kiss.

Hard. Demanding. Full of promise. Nothing in the world would have felt as good as giving in to that kiss, but the lie's sour taste had overwhelmed any bit of sweet truth in it. She planted her palms against his broad shoulders and pushed away. Cutting off their physical connection and doing her damnedest to burn the emotional one to the ground.

"That was a mistake." Had it only a day? She'd have sworn it was a decade. "I'll leave you to it. We'll send you a severance check in the mail. Drop off your keys with Hailey on the way out."

He stood less than two feet away, hands fisted at his sides, looking every bit like a man who'd lost it all. It may be just an Oscar–worthy performance, but she couldn't watch it any more.

She paused in the doorway, her chest aching. "Goodbye, Sean."

"Natalie..."

If she stayed to hear the rest, she'd crumble in front of him. She couldn't do that.

Ignoring the plea in his voice, she walked out.

Chapter Thirteen

Sitting at The Kitchen Sink's counter, Sean stared at the pecan pie slice on the bright–yellow plate. His SUV was packed and saying goodbye to Ruby Sue was the last thing he needed to do before hitting the road like he should have done yesterday. She was on the phone in the back with a supplier, so Ellen had delivered him the last slice of pie and a cup of coffee while he waited.

The pie was the perfect combination of sweet goo and crunchy nuts with a flaky crust that had to have an illegal amount of butter in it to be so damn good. Still, he couldn't make himself pick up the fork and dig into his last taste of Salvation.

Ruby Sue sidled up to him and plunked a glass of sweet tea on the counter. "You know, George Gunderson threatened to fillet Joe Haver once when he thought Joe had cut in line and stolen the last piece of my pecan pie."

That might not be such a bad way to go. It had to hurt a hell of a lot less than he did right now. "Is he around?"

"Nope." She pulled herself up into the high–backed stool on Sean's right. "You're good."

"Just my luck." He picked up the fork and poked at the crust, flaking off a few pieces and then using the back of the fork to grind them into dust.

Ruby Sue patted him on the shoulder. "Buck up, you'll be back at the brewery before you know it."

He froze. And here he figured he was getting out of Dodge fast enough to beat the wildfire of gossip. "How did you know?"

She cackled and poured three sugar packets into her already sweetened tea. "Boy, who do you think you're you talking to? This town talks as fast as a sinner during a deathbed confession." She nodded. "So can the moping and eat this pie before folks start saying I've lost my touch."

"You have it." He slid the pie over to her. "The real reason I came in was to say goodbye."

Ruby Sue ignored the pie and narrowed her eyes. "Why would you do that?"

"I packed up my stuff and gave the house a quick once–over." He dropped the keys to the house on the counter. "I know I was supposed to give you two months' notice, but I'm sure you won't have trouble finding a new renter. I left it furnished."

"I see." No one would ever call Ruby Sue soft and cushy, but she went completely rigid. She shoved her glass away and turned to give him her full attention. The look of utter disgust on her face gutted him.

He didn't know what he'd expected Ruby Sue's reaction to be to his announcement, but an eight on a ten–point pissed–off scale wasn't it. Like his own grandmother, Ruby Sue had cared about him when there really wasn't a reason to. He'd never be able to pay her back, but he'd be forever grateful.

Easing down from the stool, he couldn't go without asking one more favor. "Look, I know you're close to the Sweet triplets. There's something going on over at the brewery and the local deputies don't seem to be all that concerned about it. If there's any way you could put a bug in the sheriff's ear, that would be a huge help."

She held out her arm like a queen reaching out to a footman. Without a second thought, he took her hand and helped her down from her seat.

Once on her feet, she planted her hands on her hips and looked up at him with fire in her eyes. "So you're telling me there's trouble and you're just hightailing it out of town faster than the roadrunner in one of those cartoons."

Yes, and in his spare time he plucked the wings off butterflies and told small children that Santa didn't exist. "It's not ideal, I know. I'm sorry."

"You sure are sorry."

"Ruby Sue—"

"Don't you Ruby Sue me." She huffed out a breath. "I don't know how you ended up here in Salvation, but the good Lord brought you here for a reason and you're a damn fool to leave now just because you ran into a little roadblock."

As if it was that simple. "Natalie fired me."

"As she should have. That girl loves her rules, always has. She was one of those kids who would chew each bite exactly thirty–two times." She poked a bony finger into his ribs. "You lied to her. She called you on it. And instead of acting like a man and trying to make up for it, you turned chickenshit."

Ouch. Fighting with Ruby Sue was like trading jabs with a boxer way above his weight class. "Not fair."

"Waah." She imitated a baby rubbing her eyes. "Life isn't fair. Grow up and deal with it." She crossed her arms and shot him a hard look. "You made a life here in Salvation—a good one. Maybe instead of running away from something, you should be running *toward* someone."

Okay, he loved the batty old woman, but he'd had enough. He didn't need anyone telling him what to do with his life. It was his to fuck up if he damn well wanted to. "I don't need to hear this."

Ruby Sue snorted. "It's exactly what you need to hear and you know it."

"It's been nice knowing you." Sean stormed out the door—

And right into Rupert Crowley's blinding spotlight.

Fuck. Just when he thought his life couldn't get any worse, the man who'd stalked him for almost a decade had finally cornered him. Anger unspooled inside him and it took everything he had not to punch Crowley right in the nose.

The reporter stood with a single camera operator between Sean and his SUV. Rupert shoved a microphone in Sean's face. "Sean Duvin, you've been living off the grid in a small town for years. What made you choose Salvation?"

It took every last bit of self–control he had, but Sean brushed past the reporter and his camera operator to his SUV.

Never one to give up, Crowley dogged Sean's footsteps. "Your fans want to know why you left and what happened."

"No comment," Sean ground out between clenched teeth as he yanked open the driver's side door.

He hopped in, hit the door locks, and started the engine. Glancing up, he spotted Ruby Sue and Ellen standing in The Kitchen Sink's doorway.

Whatever he'd expected to be his last sight of Salvation, this wasn't it.

The older woman stood with her arms wrapped tight around her middle, tears running down her face. Ellen had an arm around Ruby Sue's frail shoulders and a sad little smile on her face. She lifted her free hand to wave goodbye and mouthed the words "Good luck."

At that moment, he would have welcomed a kick in the balls rather than the ache racking him.

Rupert knocked on the SUV's window, pulling Sean's attention. The reporter opened his mouth but Sean gunned the engine, drowning out whatever the man had to say.

Running was the only option Sean had left. He didn't have a choice. If he was still here when Rupert aired his report, it would only be a matter of time before his father found him, and he never wanted to see that bastard again in his life.

Pulling out onto Main Street, he gave The Kitchen Sink one last look in the rear–view mirror. A dark–blue baseball cap tossed on the backseat showed in the mirror's lower right corner. He didn't have to look closer to know it had Sweet Salvation Brewery embroidered on it in red.

Well, he didn't need that thing anymore. There were other jobs out there. He'd hire on with a construction crew or he'd go back to bussing tables. Maybe he'd finally empty the millions out of his Hollywood bank account before disappearing again—this time for good. Hell, he might as well take the money and run. He's was a damn fool for not draining the account sooner and killing off the ghosts of his old life.

Turning left onto Highway 28, he blew past the Salvation City Limits sign and the Fix 'Er Up Auto Body Shop. Driving into the early darkness, he squinted to make out the signs for the upcoming interstate alongside the highway. The interstate would take him as far north or south as he wanted to go. It didn't matter which exit he took as long as it got him out of Salvation and away from reminders of Natalie.

How many miles would that take?

More than this road had.

He eased his foot off the gas pedal. An eighteen-wheeler's driver blared his horn and whizzed around Sean's SUV. He didn't even flinch. All he could hear was Ruby Sue's pointed statement. Was he running away from something when he should be running toward someone?

Toward Natalie.

A quarter mile went by.

The scent of honeysuckle snuck into the SUV.

Then another quarter mile.

He could hear her soft moans.

And another quarter mile.

The road disappeared and all he could see was her light–brown waves tumbling down around her shoulders.

He coasted down the interstate's shoulder until finally, his SUV puttered to a stop in front of an exit ramp. The farther he went, the closer he got to her. It didn't make sense, but he couldn't deny the truth of it.

Flipping on the hazard lights, he stared at the green sign with the four–letter word in large white block letters: Exit.

Certainty slammed into him.

He was done running. He'd been done the moment Natalie had walked into his life with her cotton–candy sweaters, tiny little buttons and ever–present clipboard full of change.

Now it was time to prove it to her.

An interloper in what had been his sanctuary, Sean skulked through the Sweet Salvation Brewery's front doors like a trespasser. He'd been counting on the brewery's tasting room being abandoned in the few minutes before everything shut down for the night. The fates must have been smiling down at him because there wasn't a soul to be seen as he pocketed the keys he was supposed to have left with Hailey yesterday.

Natalie's subcompact was still in the parking lot, so he knew she was here. He had to find her and explain everything. It may not get him his job back, but that wasn't his number–one priority right now. Shit, it hadn't been since Natalie had come into his life. She'd changed everything and he hadn't even realized until now.

Turning the corner into the hallway leading to Natalie's office, he almost plowed into Billy. "Whoa, sorry about that, kid."

"What are you doing here?" Billy looked over his shoulder. "Miranda and Natalie made the announcement this morning that you were...uh..."

Feeling sorry for the kid, he threw him a bone. "Fired?"

Billy stared at his tennis shoes. "I was gonna say let go."

"That's a nicer way of putting it."

"Oh God." Billy's eyes rounded and his gaze bounced all around Sean. "You're not gonna do something crazy are you?"

Understanding why Billy might be on edge, Sean held up his hands, palms forward, showing he wasn't armed. "Nope, but I have to talk to Natalie."

Billy gave him a smirky smile. "I'd heard rumors about you two. Come on." He turned and headed toward the brewery floor.

Following close behind, Sean shook his head. "Is there anyone in Salvation who doesn't gossip?"

He shrugged. "It's a small town. We're each other's entertainment." Billy pushed open one of the swinging doors that led to the brewery floor. "Natalie and Miranda sent everyone home early tonight, I guess to make up for canning you. She's in the research room."

"Thanks, man." Sean slipped through the opening.

Billy gave him a thumbs–up. "Good luck, man. I'll lock the front door behind myself."

Crossing the brewery floor, his footsteps echoed in the empty, cavernous space.

He'd never been this nervous in his life. Not when he'd stood up to his father and his angry fists for the first time. Not when he'd skipped town with a few bucks in his pocket and a stolen car. Not when he'd first walked into The Kitchen Sink hungry, exhausted, and lost to ask Ruby Sue for a job—any job. None of those snapshots in time mattered as much as this.

He paused just outside the reference room and spied her from the doorway.

Natalie stood with her back to him, reading through his notes for the sweet–and–sour stout that would win the Southern Brewers Invitational. Hair pulled back into a ponytail and wearing her signature cardigan–and–skirt combo, she looked so much like she had the first day he'd seen her. That day he'd pegged her as an uptight micromanager with a phenomenal ass and then proceeded to spend the first few weeks ignoring her completely.

What a fucking idiot.

"Natalie."

She whipped around, her fingers clutching her pearl necklace. As soon as she saw him, the surprise faded from her blue eyes, replaced by a much cooler emotion. "What are you doing here?"

Walking in with his hands up, he stopped a few feet away from her. "We need to talk."

"No, we don't." She pushed her glasses up her nose and inhaled a shaky breath.

"I owe you an explanation." He tried to think of a decent counterargument for when she told him to shove off.

She considered him for a moment, her jaw tight as she rubbed her upper arms. "If that's what it takes to get you to leave, let's hear it."

Surprised, his mind went blank. Shit. What did he do now?

While he fumbled for words, for where to begin, she stared, not giving him an inch. He took a deep breath. As Julie Andrews said, the beginning is a very good place to start.

“My dad was a frustrated actor who’d never gotten his big break, so he was determined to make his son a success. I started going on auditions as soon as I could sit up on my own. Commercials led to television shows, which led to movies.”

“Don’t forget the Oscar.” A hurt bitterness twisted her tone.

Damn, he had fucked this up so bad. He hated that he’d done that to her. “Yeah, and an Oscar. Rupert got parts of the story right. I was wild. I did things I shouldn’t have and took advantage of people whose only goal was to be with someone famous.”

Those days were hazy, but the ugly loneliness came through in crisp detail. It still had the power to rake its claws through his flesh and leave a gaping wound that never seemed to heal.

“But it caught up to you,” Natalie prompted.

If only it had been that easy. “No.” Sean shook his head. “My father caught up to me. He had a wicked backhand but when I was younger he’d usually made sure to land the real nasty blows on places that the camera wouldn’t pick up. Forgotten lines might mean a swift smack the first time. The second time resulted in the whistle of his belt. If I fucked–up a third time, I’d spend the night in the closet. Being a child actor wasn’t fun and games for me. It was a way of keeping my dad appeased. He controlled everything I did and every hour of my day.”

Her hand covered her mouth in horror. “My God, how long did it go on?”

“Until I got big enough to fight back.” He shrugged. “Those are the days when I’d report to the set early so the makeup artists would have time to cover the bruises. They figured I was just another head case with too much money and fame, running wild. I never bothered to correct them."

Natalie crossed the room. Her gentle fingers brushed the scar above his eye from when his father had launched a coffee cup at him. "I'm so sorry, Sean." She rose up on her tiptoes, kissed the scar, and stepped back.

He hated losing her touch, but he had to finish. It couldn't be only about pity for him. "That wasn't the worst of what my father had done. My mom had taken off shortly after I was born. So it had been just my dad and I. When I was eighteen, my grandmother moved to California. She lived nearby, but not close enough to see what was going on. Ruby Sue reminds me of her—a deadly combination of brass–knuckle tough love served with a side of cookies. At that time, I wanted nothing more than to retire from acting, but my dad was dead set against it. Once I'd gotten too big to beat, he had to learn other ways to keep me in line and acting."

She took his hand in hers and squeezed. "What happened?"

"My grandmother got sick." His voice broke. He closed his eyes and saw her frail and helpless in the hospital, too weak to complain but too strong to let go. "Really sick. And my bastard of a father, her own son, used her care as a bargaining chip. He'd found a script and thought I'd be perfect for it. If I didn't agree to take the part, my grandmother would go from her expensive but exceptional nursing facility to a state–run place. He was her legal guardian at that point and had total control over where she lived."

It wasn't until the bastard had offered that ultimatum that Sean really learned how deep his hate could go. "I took the part. She stayed where she was, but she didn't get better. She died a week before the Academy Awards."

Natalie brought his hand to her soft lips and kissed him. The gentle reminder of her presence saving him from falling down the rabbit hole of painful memories.

"I don't remember a damn thing about the awards ceremony until I was up on that stage. I stared down at my father with so much hatred in my heart that I wanted to kill the bastard right there on national television. Instead, as soon as I got offstage, I gave him the statue and snuck out the back. I stole a car and started running. I didn't stop until I got to Salvation. Everything about me here started out as a lie, but I swear to God that lie helped me find the truth. It helped me find you." The gossipy little town had saved him and falling in love with Natalie had set him free. "So that's it. Now you know everything."

"Do you ever miss acting?" she asked, her eyes swimming with emotion.

He almost told her no, just so to make those unshed tears disappear. But he was done lying to Natalie. "Only when I remember that feeling of being totally free and losing myself in a role. Sure, it was just glorified pretending, but I was good at it and a part of me still loved it despite my father."

"Sean—" A blaring alarm went off in the brewery. Red lights flashed and the emergency lighting flipped on. "What the hell?"

He pulled Natalie close, adrenaline shooting through his veins. The saboteur, it had to be. "Power outage."

"How?" She moved toward the research room's door and reached for the knob.

"Not how, *who.*" He moved ahead of her, standing between her and the door. "Stay in here and keep the door locked."

Pulling her close, he lowered his mouth to her soft lips. There wasn't time to tell her everything else he wanted to say, but he was never good with words that didn't come from a script anyway. All he could give her was himself and pray like hell it was enough. He ended the kiss and sprinted out of the room, determined to find the asshole fucking with the brewery before he could do more damage—or worse, hurt Natalie.

Shadows filled most of the brewery floor. As he hustled toward the electric panel to throw on the lights, a human–shaped shadow peeled away from the gloom.

He saw the flash before he heard the gun's crack.

The bullet tore through his upper arm, knocking him off his feet. Falling backward, his head hit the concrete hard and bounced twice before an inky blackness fell.

Chapter Fourteen

Natalie grabbed an empty beer growler from the shelf and ran out into the dark before the gunshot finished echoing. She had to get to Sean before whoever was out there got him, if she wasn't already too late.

Adrenaline shot through her veins as she hurried as fast as she could through the brewery. The fermentation tanks, brew kettles, and tall stacks of malt and barley loomed high, casting shadows in the soft–red emergency lighting that spanned most of the concrete floor. Visibility for shit, she slowed her pace, searching for Sean in the darkness.

Her pulse pounded in her ears, almost as loud as her panicked breathing. A staticky white noise buzzed in her head and her lungs pinched closed as the panic attack hit with thunderous effect. The sudden lack of oxygen knocked her to her knees. She hit the concrete floor, pain jolting up from her kneecaps, and she cried out. Unable to get more than a sip of air into her lungs at a time, her chest burned.

"You weren't supposed to be here, but it looks like I'm the lucky one tonight." Low and mean, the voice stabbed its way through the static blaring in Natalie's head. "Get up or I'll just shoot you here."

A foot slammed into her side and she winced. Fighting against the blackness, she didn't reach for the pearls. She didn't have to. A vision of Sean out there somewhere, needing her help, brought light back to darkness and oxygen into her lungs. She wouldn't let the anxiety win if that meant losing Sean.

"Come on," the voice ordered. "I don't have all night."

Gritting her teeth, Natalie pressed her hands to the cool concrete and pushed herself up. Once upright, she took a good look at her attacker—and realized she had no fucking clue who it was. "Who are you?"

The woman had golden–blonde hair arranged in a complicated updo that would make a Miss America contestant jealous. Her makeup was flawless and she wore head–to–toe black, like a cartoon version of a cat burglar. "Joni Brennan. I believe you know my husband."

Shock cut through the panic eating away at the edges of her vision. "You're Carl's wife?"

"The one and only." Joni raised an all–steel .357 Magnum with a three–inch barrel and aimed it right at Natalie's head.

Her heart almost stopped in her chest. "Where's Sean?"

"Start moving and I'll take you to him." Joni clicked off the gun's safety. "Gotta tell you though, he's probably not worth it. Look at *me*. I bet all my chips on that son of a bitch Carl, and I lost. Big. It turns out my parents were right. I didn't marry a man with potential. I hitched my wagon to a mean drunk with illusions of grandeur. I became a laughingstock." She shoved the gun in Natalie's back and pushed her forward. "You of all people should understand the horror of that. You're a Sweet, after all."

Refusing to surrender to the anxiety still eating away at the back of her brain, Natalie took a step forward and then another. If she could keep Joni talking, the other woman might get comfortable enough to let down her guard. It wasn't much, but it was the only plan Natalie could come up with on short notice.

"What does that have to do with the brewery?"

"Everything," the woman snarled. "The Sweet Salvation Brewery was supposed to be ours." She pushed Natalie around a corner. "Instead, you three bitches come along and steal it right from under us. Owning this brewery and making it a success would have shown my family and the rest of this town that they were wrong."

Natalie tripped over something solid at her feet. Desperate to stay upright, she grabbed the first thing her flailing arms encountered: Clyde's workbench. Her knees cracked against the concrete floor but the move kept her from falling straight down.

That's when she saw it. Saw *him*. The red emergency lighting outlined Sean's motionless body at her feet.

The world came to a standstill as an entire lifetime of what if and now never will be ran through her mind. She'd come to Salvation to solve the problem of Natalie and find her own happily ever after. And for a minute, she had. She hated Sean's lies, but after hearing his explanation understood why he'd done it. He'd been fighting for control just as much as she had. What had he said? That she hated change she couldn't control? Well, she sure as hell hadn't been able to control her feelings for Sean. She'd fallen in love and now it was too late. Every part of her ached with regret.

Then Sean's chest rose with a shaky breath and she nearly sank to the floor with relief.

When they got out of this alive, she was going to kill him for running into the brewery as though he had a stunt double around the corner to take the hits.

"Come on, klutz," Joni ordered.

Every ounce of worry and fear drained out of her, replaced with a rage ocean–deep and mountain–wide, with only one target. Palming a wrench, Natalie slid it up the sleeve of her sweater and straightened.

Her first instinct was the strike out immediately, but she knew she couldn't. If she had any hope of taking Joni out, she had to time it just right.

She kept her hand close to her thigh and continued forward. "Does Carl know?"

"That idiot? Of course not." The emotionless cold in Joni's voice added an extra bit of creepy to the whole fucked–up situation. "When he got out on bail after running your sister off the road, I bailed him out, got him drunk and kept him that way so he missed his court appearance. And while he was passed out, I made sure things started going wrong here. Now, I never expected him to shoot himself after I spiked his morning whiskey with PCP, but the unexpected happens and you have to deal with it."

"You set him up," Natalie prompted, leading Joni farther away from Sean.

"A nice little bit of irony there, wasn't it? Of course, I didn't expect law enforcement to be so dead set against actually investigating the accidents." She jabbed the revolver into Natalie's back. "That's far enough."

Swallowing her fear, Natalie put everything she had into remaining calm. "Carl's in jail, you won't be able to blame him for this."

"True, but the sheriff's deputies aren't much interested in investigating the goings on at the Sweet Salvation Brewery, are they? They'll tie the explosion to a gas leak and it'll be just another horrible accident at a poorly run craft brewery that resulted in two people's deaths." Joni took a step back. "Too bad for you it had to end like this."

Using every trick and tip she'd ever learned from Dr. Kenning, Natalie marshaled all of her focus and intent into this moment.

She inhaled a deep breath and let the wrench drop into her palm.

Tightening her grip around the metal hidden behind her back, she centered her weight on the balls of her feet.

The ominous sound of a safety being pulled back sounded.

"No." Natalie spun on her heel, bringing the wrench up at the same time.

The move startled Joni and she fired, but the sit went wide.

Natalie brought the wrench down with all her strength.

It cracked against the other woman's shoulder.

The gun fell and clattered against the floor, skittering into the shadows toward Sean.

Before Natalie could even make a play for the weapon, Joni screamed like a woman possessed and came at her.

A shot cracked.

Joni went down in a crumpled heap to the ground, howling, "You shot me in the ass."

Behind Joni, Sean stood with the gun. "Are you okay?"

The words were no sooner out of his mouth than he collapsed to the ground, blood streaming down his arm.

Three hours later, the hospital was a mad house. TV crews and tabloid reporters had swarmed the Salvation County Medical Complex like a plague of locusts. The news had gone viral when Rupert Crowley had breathlessly reported on the shooting at the brewery on the country's highest–rated cable news program. Everyone from the doctors to the sheriff's deputies working crowd control were talking about how Sean O'Dell was really Hollywood heartthrob Sean Duvin, who'd disappeared six years ago moments after accepting his Oscar, never to be heard from again until now.

Really, it was the best piece of gossip Salvation had whispered about in decades.

And Natalie didn't give a rat's ass. She needed to lay eyes on Sean and confirm what the paramedics had said about his condition. A concussion and minor gunshot wound were serious, but they were a helluva lot better than getting blown sky–high in a gas explosion, as Joni had planned.

Fresh from a mind–numbing interrogation by law enforcement, Natalie and Miranda elbowed their way through the crowd to the hospital's front doors.

"There she is," someone hollered. "It's Natalie Sweet."

A platoon of cameras turned in her direction. Reporters rushed forward en masse, shoving microphones in her face and yelling questions at her.

"Are you sleeping with Sean Duvin?"

"Did Sean save your life?"

"Will you move back to California with him?"

"Is it true he has a harem living with him?"

"Did you lie to the police to protect his identity?"

"Are you his biggest fan?"

Natalie shrank back from the blazing lights and the deafening noise. Her chest tightened, squeezing all the oxygen from her lungs. The buzzing blared in her head.

Just when she thought she was going to crumple, her sister grabbed her hand and yanked her through the hospital's front doors.

Miranda pulled her into a quiet waiting room with its florescent lights, white–tiled floors, and heavy scent of disinfectant. "You okay, sis?"

Natalie fought to calm her breathing before she hyperventilated. In. She pictured Sean's face as he told her about the stout he was making for the invitational. Out. The feel of his fingers as he tucked her hair behind her ear. In. The sound of her name coming from his lips. Out. The way he looked at her as if she was his and always had been. Her heart rate slowed and the hospital waiting room came back into focus.

She gave her sister a thumbs–up. "Better."

"Good. You stay here where the jackals can't see you. I'll go find out Sean's room number." Miranda marched off to the nurse's station.

Relieved not to have to see the crowd anymore, Natalie sank down into a chair. How ridiculous was it that she could face down a deranged woman intent on blowing up the Sweet Salvation Brewery, but couldn't handle the shouting reporters gathered outside?

"It's horrible how they behave, isn't it?" A thin, balding man sitting in the corner spoke up. "I told Sean I think it will only get worse now that the press has found him."

Salvation was a small town. While she may not know every person by name, she knew pretty much all of them by sight, and this guy in his ironed designer jeans and blinged–out T–shirt with a tiger on it was definitely not local.

Wary of another sneak attack by a reporter, Natalie stiffened. "Who are you?"

"Sorry, it's been a crazy day and I think I left my manners somewhere above Iowa." He gave her a friendly wave. "I'm Hartley, Sean's former manager. And you must the Natalie that Sean told me all about. I flew in this afternoon, after I heard the scuttlebutt that Rupert Crowley had found him. I wanted to warn Sean that the swarm outside was coming, but it looks like I was too late." He shook his head. "At least he'll have better protection from their prying eyes once he gets back home to California."

Her heart stuttered to a stop. "He's leaving Salvation?"

Natalie knew she shouldn't be surprised. She'd fired him. Told him to get out of her life and stay out. He'd only come back to the brewery tonight to explain himself. That was all. It didn't mean he wanted to stay. It sure as hell didn't mean he wanted her. She glanced out the window at the press milling around outside. Especially not after he'd been found.

"Yes. He asked me to book him a one–way ticket. Who knows, maybe in time he'll try acting again. He really is talented. I'm already getting offers e–mailed to me."

What did Salvation have to offer in comparison besides a rundown brewery, a town full of people who loved nothing more than being all up in everyone else's business, and her. She didn't need a flowchart to demonstrate that it wasn't enough.

"I hope everything works out just like he wants." She squeezed out the words before anguish sealed off her throat with a lump the size of Texas.

"It can be hard for people to get the business completely out of their system—especially someone with as much talent and drive as Sean. But I'm sure he'll call. Maybe even come back for a visit sometime. It seems like an...interesting little town." Hartley spoke softly with the gentle understanding of a favorite uncle explaining that unicorns weren't real. "After all, Hollywood specializes in happy endings."

But Salvation didn't. Not for her. She'd come back here to figure out what was wrong with her and why she'd relationship blocked herself. Now, thanks to Sean, she knew. Maybe the solution wasn't to hold on so tight, but to finally let go—like he already had.

Usually a research breakthrough like this was cause for celebration. Not this time. The epiphany couldn't block out the misery winding around her heart like a python and squeezing until it cracked. She couldn't see Sean like this. If she did, she'd break right in half and probably beg him to stay. That was no way to repay him for teaching her such a valuable lesson. He deserved better than a half–broken girl in a podunk town. He deserved the Hollywood ending and she loved him too much to deny him that.

Miranda strode into the waiting room. "The old witch at the front desk says visiting hours are over."

Holding on to what little bit of control over her emotions remained after Hartley's revelations, Natalie grabbed her purse off the chair. "Tell Sean I wish him luck."

Without a second glance back, she rushed from the room and out into the cold night.

The next morning, Sean blinked against the bright florescent light, bringing his hospital room into focus. White walls. White sheets. White bandages covering his left biceps. The doctors had insisted on keeping him overnight to monitor him because of the probable concussion he'd suffered.

Someone cleared their throat.

He smiled. He'd been waiting for Natalie to show up.

He turned his head. A man stood on the opposite side of the room in a God–awful tiger T–shirt and six–hundred–dollar jeans. He looked familiar.

"Who—" Sean started, then the first hint of Old Spice hit him. "Get the fuck out."

Hartley Duvin smiled through clenched teeth. "Now is that any way to great your father and manager?"

Instead of the looming, larger–than–life man of horrible rages, his father appeared to be just another average Joe. Thin. Balding. More than a little worn around the edges, but an underlying edge of cruelty remained.

Sean's past rushed over him in a tidal wave of anger and frustration. It overwhelmed the dull ache in his injured arm and the throbbing making his vision blurry. "You have no right to call yourself my father."

"You know how I feel about ugly talk, Sean," his old man growled, as if he still had the power to force Sean into submission. He'd lost that ability the day Sean's grandmother had died, and the old man didn't have anything to hold over his son's head anymore. "There's an entire media circus set up outside the hospital doors waiting to hear what it's like to finally see my long–lost son, who just happened to foil a criminal plot. Just like in one of your films. I fully expect a spike in demand for your old movies and memorabilia. Of course, I'll get me a cut of the profits, since I was your manager at the time of their release."

Sean sank back against the thin hospital pillow. It made sense. He had never been anything but a breathing paycheck to his father. A means to his own little slice of celebrity. "Crowley told you where I was?"

The tabloid reporter and his father were like two peas in a pod when it came to exploitation.

"Yes, we've become friends over the years. He called me two days ago, and I came all the way across the country to this godforsaken town as soon as I could."

Sean didn't doubt his dad would travel the world three times over if the payday was right. "What will it take to get you to leave?"

"You on the plane right next to me, with everything timed for our arrival at L.A.X. for full paparazzi effect."

Sean rolled his eyes. "That's not happening. Ever."

His dad responded without hesitating. "It will or else that small–town girl of yours will find herself paying for your stubbornness."

Sean sat up so fast his head felt as if were going to roll off his neck. "What did you do?"

"Nothing really. Not yet anyway." That old mean–as–sin glint that had always made Sean's blood run cold sparkled in his father's eyes. "Of course, I did break it to her that you were made for bigger things than just some penny–ante brewery. I already have several scripts for you to take a look at."

Sean's vision blackened with anger. He was up and out of the hospital bed in a heartbeat. Grabbing his father by the collar, he pulled him close and saw something he never had before.

Fear in his father's eyes.

"You don't touch Natalie, the brewery, or anyone in this town. You do and I'll hunt you down like a dog. The authorities will never find what's left of you after I get done."

His old man squirmed in his grasp, but he wasn't going anywhere. "Is that how you learned to treat your betters in this shithole little town?"

Sean slammed his father against the wall, grabbing his throat and lifting until the old man's toes barely touched the floor. He leaned in close, not wanting his father to miss a single fucking word of what he was going to say. "I learned a helluva lot more here in Salvation than I ever did from you. I learned how to treat people. I learned that not everyone is just in it for themselves. I learned how to be a man."

"That's fucking touching." Hartley spit out the words as the tips of his toes tapped the floor, no doubt looking for a high spot to relieve the pressure on his neck. "I might cry."

Something inside Sean snapped. All the rage he'd built up over a lifetime exploded to the surface and he pressed his hand against the old man's Adam's apple. A little extra pressure—one solid push—and the bones would snap. His father's eyes bulged and his face turned red.

Power. Control. Fury. They ran through Sean's blood like a runaway train and he relished the frightened look in his father's watering eyes. It would be easy to end it all here. Like this.

He increased the pressure just enough so his father danced on the edge of life and death. How many times had their roles been reversed and his father had him pinned to a wall, wondering if this was it? Too many to count.

Unbridled hatred. That was the lesson his father had passed down to his son, and it wasn't until this moment that Sean realized he'd learned it so well.

"Salvation taught me a lot, but it was Natalie that showed me the most important thing of all—the kind of person I want to be. And that person is not you." He let go. His father dropped to the ground, sputtering, sucking in great lungsful of air. "Get the fuck out of here and don't ever come back."

Like cowards everywhere, his father wilted when confronted. He scurried to the door and paused. "You'll regret this."

"No. I won't." Sean sat back down on the bed, but didn't relax until the door swished shut.

And to think he'd been running for years from that sad parody of a father. What a fucking waste of time and energy. Time to start putting all that to better use. He picked up the phone and called the brewery. He needed to talk to Natalie, and knowing her, she was five points into a thirty–point plan for cleaning up the mess from last night.

"Sweet Salvation Brewery," Hailey's cheerful voice chirped.

"Hi, Hailey, it's Sean. Is Natalie there?"

An awkward silence fell. "Sorry, she's not available. Can I take a message?"

Fuck. Whatever his father had really told Natalie must have been horrible. "What's going on, Hailey?"

"Don't put me in this spot," she pleaded.

"Please." A single word more powerful than just about any other he knew.

"She said not to put any of your calls through. I'm sorry." The dial tone sounded in his ear.

He'd had a lifetime to build up his defenses when it came to the mind games his father played. But Natalie hadn't. The old man had probably homed in on every perceived weakness and pushed as hard as he could in a short span of time.

What did Natalie always say, find a problem, fix a problem? Well he had one hell of a problem and he was going to do whatever it took to fix it.

Sean closed his eyes. Ignoring the pain racking his body, he did the one thing he'd never done before. He reached for the phone and called the man who'd led his father to him. Rupert Crowley owed him one—and he was going to deliver.

"Hello?" Crowley answered.

"You called my father."

The reporter hemmed and hawed for a second. "Reunion stories are killer for the ratings. Come on, you're in the business. You know this."

The one benefit of being raised by a master manipulator was knowing how to focus right in on what made people tick. When it came to Crowley, that was easy. "What would an exclusive interview with me do for your ratings?"

Chapter Fifteen

A jittery sensation Sean hadn't felt since before he'd stepped onstage to accept his Oscar buzzed through his body, leaving him anxious and unfocused.

"You ready?" Rupert adjusted his camera for the thousandth time. "We go live in a minute. No second takes on this one."

"I'm good." Sean stood on his mark and closed his eyes.

It was an old trick his first acting teacher had taught him: To center himself prior to a take, an actor closed his eyes and pictured the calmest place he could think of and then added in the other sensory details—the smell, sounds, taste, and feeling of it.

He didn't know what others pictured; maybe it was a beach or field of flowers or some crazy shit. Sean had always pictured the stage of whatever set he was on. He may not have ever had a choice in being a child actor, but being on the set under the bright lights was the only place his father couldn't get to him with a careless backhand or a vicious remark. It was his safe place.

With a deep exhale, he cleared away the darkness behind his eyelids and revealed an empty stage. On the next heartbeat he added the director, the camera operators and the sound guy. He inhaled the fresh–paint scent of newly finished sets, felt the heat from the Klieg lights and heard the muffled footsteps of the extras waiting on the edge of the soundstage. Everything was in place, but it remained ephemeral and hazy, like a half–remembered dream.

Sweat dampened his palms and a jittery breath broke the mental image into a hundred pieces. Once again he stood alone in his mind's eye. He couldn't fall to stage fright. Not now. There wasn't going to be a second take, he had to get it right the first time. Everything depended on it. Fisting his hands, Sean tried again.

But instead of a stage, he stood in the Sweet Salvation Brewery. Billy, Hailey, Miranda, and all the others were on the edges of his vision, but it was Natalie who stood next to him, with her clipboard and her sweater with all those tiny buttons. He inhaled her honeysuckle scent, felt the softness of her creamy skin and heard the way she called his name in the throes of passion.

Immediately, his nerves faded in comparison to Natalie's high–definition image.

After a final look at the woman who'd become his everything, Sean opened his eyes.

The camera light blinked on.

Safe in her pristine white office at the Sweet Salvation Brewery, Natalie ran her fingers across the smooth pearls around her neck. For years she'd restored a sense of calm by tracing the round orbs, but today was the first time since she put it on years ago that she felt for the gold clasp. Pinching her fingers together, she grasped it and popped it open. The necklace slid from her neck and clattered to the desk.

She held her breath, waiting for the beginnings of an anxiety attack—the static in her brain, the tightening in her lungs and the blurring in her vision.

It never came.

The horrible ache in her heart remained, but the pearl necklace couldn't do a damn thing to repair that. She didn't have a flowchart or an organizational system to fix it either. And for once, she was okay with that. She'd finally taken Max's advice and made change her bitch. Mostly.

Her office door slammed open and Miranda tore across the room, skidding to a stop next to Natalie's chair. "Go to *Hollywood and Vine Reports*."

"Why should I?" She swept her necklace into her top drawer, not ready to discuss the change yet, not even with her sister.

Miranda shot her an epic–level side eye. "They're going to be live–streaming it, and it's live on three of the cable news networks too." She grabbed Natalie's keyboard. "Here, let me."

Sean appeared on the computer screen in a close–up shot and her pulse kicked up to heavy cardio levels. He'd shaved his beard, revealing a square jaw with a dimpled chin, and he'd ditched his Sweet Salvation Brewery hat. His wavy hair was artfully tousled and his leather jacket emphasized the dangerous edge to his rugged good looks.

There was no denying who he was now. Sean O'Dell was gone.

And she was glad. Really. Fucking. Glad.

She ripped her gaze away from the screen and bit down on her quivering bottom lip. Her throat tightened with emotion that threatened to spill over and she blinked rapidly. "I really don't want to see him—"

"It's about to start. Why isn't your sound working?" Miranda grabbed the mouse and clicked several times until she got the volume where she wanted it.

"So Sean, what happened?" Rupert asked.

Sean looked directly into the camera, but it was as if he were looking right at Natalie. She couldn't stop the quaking in her shoulders as the tears came down.

"I've spent most of my life pretending to be someone else," Sean said. "In the beginning it was pretending to be the perfect son to avoid my father's fists. I got good enough at faking it that people started to pay me to be someone else. I liked it. It was easier than figuring out who I was. But all of it caught up with me and I realized on that stage, with that gold statue in my hand, that I'd been pretending for so long, I had no idea what was real."

"So you disappeared," Rupert said from off screen. "Your father was your manager, but even he didn't know where you went."

"No."

"I see." Rupert paused for dramatic effect. "Doesn't seem like there's much love lost."

Sean just gave him the patented shut–up–and–you'll–live–keep–talking–and–you–die dirty look. Natalie clasped her hands together in her lap to keep from reaching through her computer screen to smack the obnoxious reporter upside the head.

Rupert cleared his throat. “You’ve done a lot to avoid the press, your family, and anyone tied to the entertainment industry. Why agree to this interview now?”

The camera operator zoomed in on Sean’s face. Natalie stopped breathing and her hand flew to her neck. The pearls were gone, but old habits died hard.

“Because I’m done running.” The camera pulled back, showing the Sweet Salvation Brewery sign that Sean stood in front of. “My name is Sean Duvin. I don’t have a lot to recommend me. I’ve lied to the people I care about. I’ll probably never want to sit around and talk about my feelings. I’m a slob. I like to fly by the seat of my pants. But I love you, Natalie Sweet. I love your button–up sweaters, the fact that you’re always talking, and your damn clipboard. I love that you make a plan for everything and that your contingency plans have contingency plans. From this day forward, I promise I’ll never hurt you. I’ll never pretend with you. I’ll never lie to you. I’ll always love you.”

He might have said more, Natalie couldn’t hear over the sound of her own crying. Damn that man. He could make her ugly–cry harder than anyone she’d ever met. If this was love, it pretty much sucked.

Miranda elbowed her and handed her a tissue. “Clean yourself up, you have to go out there.”

She took the tissue with shaking hands and wiped the tears from her face. “I can’t.” She sniffled into the tissue.

“Do you love him?” Miranda asked.

She closed her eyes and saw Sean’s lazy smile. Heard his warm voice. Felt the strength and gentleness in his touch. “Yes.”

Miranda yanked Natalie out of her chair and shoved her toward the door. "Then get your ass out there before he's gone."

Her feet wouldn't move and everything inside her was a jumbled mess, making her float and sink at the same time. "I'm scared."

"Of course you are." Miranda gave her a quick, tight hug. "That's how you know it really matters."

Sean glanced at the brewery's front door. Not even a shadow moved behind it. The rejection hit him like the number–six bus and his brain stopped functioning except to register the throbbing ache in his chest.

"And is she in there?" Rupert nodded toward the brewery, nudging the camera operator so he turned the lens toward the building. "Your Natalie?"

"Yes." The single word barely made it out through the narrow opening in his constricted throat.

The three men stood there staring at the door like a pack of fools, waiting for a miracle.

Nothing.

Nothing.

Nothing.

Sean grimaced and reached for the cool detachment that had served him so well in the past. He couldn't find it. "That's a wrap." He spun on his heel and headed for his SUV.

"Wait," Rupert called, his voice rising excitedly. "The door. It's opening."

Sean turned, afraid to even hope.

The brewery door opened and Natalie walked out. She took three steps and stopped. Her nose looked a lot like Rudolph's, she clutched a tissue box to her chest, and she looked breathtakingly beautiful.

He didn't think. He just ran. Not away from his past this time, but toward his future.

She collapsed against him and he wrapped his arms around her.

He buried his face in her hair and breathed in her honeysuckle scent. "I didn't think you were going to come out."

"It took some time." She looked up at him, her blue eyes watery behind her black–framed glasses. "I don't have a flowchart for this situation."

The fact that he'd made her cry punched him in the gut. He wiped a tear away with his thumb, wishing he could make sure they never fell again. "I don't think love works like that."

She shook her head. "No, but that's okay."

He had so much to make up for, so much to say that it ate away at him. "I'm sorry about—"

Silencing him with a finger to his lips, she raised up on her tiptoes, stopping just short of his mouth. "No matter what your name is, you'll always be the man I love."

"I love you, too," he whispered against her lips.

"I know, you just told the whole world." She giggled. "You don't always say a lot, but when you do, you make a hell of a statement."

"That I do." He lowered his lips to hers and the world faded away until it was just them.

They shouldn't work. He was the chaos to her everything–in–its–place mentality—but they did. A little sweet, a little sour, they came together and made each other better.

Rupert's excited whisper broke through the haze. "Are you getting this, Phil?"

"Yep," the camera operator responded.

Making sure not to lose contact with Natalie's lips, Sean raised his hand and blocked the camera lens.

In the background, the reporter chuckled. "And that, folks, is a real–life Hollywood ending. Reporting from the Sweet Salvation Brewery, this is Rupert Crowley wishing each of you your very own happily ever after."

A Note From Avery

Hey you!

I really hope you enjoyed Sean and Natalie. Oh how I love pitting the strong and silent type against the chatty organizer. If you have a second to leave a review of Hollywood on Tap that would be awesome—you know every time a reader leaves a review Natalie gets a new pen to color code with. :)

Please stay in touch (avery@averyflynn.com), I love hearing from readers! Want to get all the latest book news? Subscribe to my newsletter, Love Goggles, for monthly prizes and more!

And don't forget to check out Enemies on Tap: Sweet Salvation 1. It's Miranda's and Logan's story and wowzers, those two are hot together.

xoxo,

Avery

Books By Avery Flynn

The Killer Style Series
High–Heeled Wonder (Killer Style 1)
This Year's Black (Killer Style 2)

Sweet Salvation Brewery Series
Enemies on Tap (Sweet Salvation Brewery 1)
Hollywood on Tap (Sweet Salvation Brewery 2)

Novellas
Betting the Billionaire
Jax and the Beanstalk Zombies

About Avery Flynn

Avery Flynn has three slightly–wild children, loves a hockey–addicted husband and is desperately hoping someone invents the coffee IV drip.

She fell in love with romance while reading Johanna Lindsey's Mallory books. It wasn't long before Avery had read through all the romance offerings at her local library. Needing a romance fix, she turned to Harlequin's four books a month home delivery service to ease the withdrawal symptoms. That worked for a short time, but it wasn't long before the local book stores' staffs knew her by name.

Avery was a reader before she was a writer and hopes to always be both. She loves to write about smartass alpha heroes who are as good with a quip as they are with their *ahem* other God–given talents. Her heroines are feisty, fierce and fantastic. Brainy and brave, these ladies know how to stand on their own two feet and knock the bad guys off theirs.

Find out more about Avery on her website, follow her on Twitter and Pinterest, like her on her Facebook page or friend her on her Facebook profile. She's also on Goodreads and BookLikes.

Join her street team, The Flynnbots, and receive special sneak peeks, prizes and early access to her latest releases!

Also, if you figure out how to send Oreos through the Internet, she'll be your best friend for life.

Contact her at avery@averyflynn.com. She'd love to hear from you!

Also by Avery Flynn

Enemies on Tap: Sweet Salvation Brewery 1

"Flynn's first novel in the is brand spanking new series is intoxicating!" – 4.5 Stars, RT Book Reviews

Enemies ...After years away, Miranda Sweet returns to Salvation, Virginia to save her family's brewery, but her fate is in the hands of her lover–turned–enemy, Logan. What's a girl to do when the only person who can help her is the man who betrayed her?

Lovers ...Logan Martin can't believe his luck when the woman who smashed his heart to smithereens walks into his bank asking for his help. What she doesn't know is that he needs the land her brewery is on––and he'll do whatever it takes to get it.

An Irresistible Combination ...Their wager becomes a battle between their attraction and their determination to win. But it's in each other's arms that they realize there might be more at stake now than their bet. With the town against the Sweet Salvation Brewery's success, Logan has to choose between what's expected of him and what he really wants...

Betting the Billionaire

"This story has it all!" – Jennifer Probst, best selling author of The Marriage Bargain

So what if Gabe Campos is a model–dating billionaire that gets Keisha Jacobs hotter than a Ferrari's engine on the straightaway? He keeps pushing her to sell her family's furniture business, but she'll never give in.

Forced by a snow storm to spend the night together, their passion ignites. The next day, however, it's back to business. The only way Keisha can save her family is to win a bet with the billionaire. But neither realizes their hearts are part of the bargain...

High–Heeled Wonder: Killer Style 1

"When a fashionista and her bodyguard get tangled up together, watch out for sizzling sex and surprising plot twists."</b – New York Times best selling author Rebecca York

Sylvie Bissette is the woman behind The High–Heeled Wonder, a must–read blog for fashionistas everywhere. Tony Falcon wouldn't know a kitten heel from a tabby cat, but when a murder investigation leads him to Sylvie, he realizes the feisty fashionista may be his best chance at catching the criminals who killed his best friend. But solving that case means going after the

people Sylvie cares about, and soon his attraction for her—and the danger she's in—has him wondering if solving the case is worth hurting the woman he can't stop fantasizing about...

This Year's Black: Killer Style 2

"Incredible writing with witty humor and scorching sex scenes. This Year's Black belongs at the top of everyone's TBR list." – New York Times bestselling author, Gina L. Maxwell

When someone embezzles millions under Devin Harris's watch, he isn't going to let the private investigator working the case go it alone—even if she is the woman who blew him away in bed and then blew him off. Allegra "Ryder" Falcon is a fighter, but just when it seems like it couldn't get any hotter between her and Devin, the case they're working takes them to a tropical paradise where the danger increases. From the catwalk to the pineapple fields, they have to work together to track down the missing millions before the thief finds—and kills—them.

Jax and the Beanstalk Zombies: Fairy True 1

"Avery Flynn leads us into a shimmering magical world with a sexy twist that is pure, unadulterated fun. I loved this story!" – Darynda Jones, NY Times Bestselling Author

You know there's trouble ahead when zombies aren't your biggest worry.

The treasure hunter...Veronica Kwon is determined to be the only person in control of her destiny. After surviving a broken engagement and turning her back on her wealthy manipulative father, she started a treasure hunting company and is ready for the adventure of a lifetime.

The ex–fiance...Jax Taylor is a Southern charmer with enough sex appeal to melt the polar ice caps. He disappeared three months before their wedding and swore he'd never cross paths with Veronica again.

The magic beanstalk...Brought together again by their dying mentor, who has found three enchanted beans, Veronica and Jax agree to an uneasy partnership. Together they'll climb a magic beanstalk to the cloud kingdom, but will their destiny be the riches they so desire, the passion they thought dead...or will the undead get them first?

CPSIA information can be obtained at www.ICGtesting.com
Printed in the USA
BVOW01s1418090315

390904BV00006B/7/P

9 780990 833512